CHOCOLATE DEAD PUDDING

A Southern Psychic Sisters Mystery

A. GARDNER

Copyright © 2018 by A. Gardner
www.gardnerbooks.com

Cover design by Annie Moril

All rights reserved. No part of this publication may be reproduced, stored in or introduced into a retrieval system, or transmitted, in any form, or by any means (electronic, mechanical, photocopying, recording, or otherwise) without the prior written permission of the copyright owner of this book.

This is a work of fiction. Names, characters, places, brands, media, and incidents are either the product of the author's imagination or are used fictitiously. Any resemblance to actual persons, living or dead, business establishments, events, or locales is entirely coincidental.

For my readers

Dear Ms. Ember Greene,

We would like to invite you to participate in our company-wide stress management challenge featuring a cash prize awarded to one lucky winner in each region. Your regional representative will present you with the contest rules. Best of luck to you.

Kind regards,
The Clairs

Chapter 1

For the first time in her life, my sister Stevie was on a date with a vampire.

For the first time in a long time, my sister Stevie was on a *date*. Period.

"Hot wings for the table." Red's new bartender, Marlow, placed the appetizer in front of me.

Thad casually raised his hand. "Excuse me, does that sauce contain garlic?"

"Hilarious. Have you been waiting all night to use that line?" Junior rolled his eyes.

Marlow narrowed her eyes, glancing at all four of us one at a time.

"Ignore him," I said. "Thanks for the wings."

"Okay." Marlow forced a friendly smile and quickly tended to the next table.

The four of us were on a double date, and it wasn't going well. I'd had high hopes when I'd set it all up. It was a well-known fact that our new neighbor Junior had a thing for my sister. It was also a well-known fact that my sister was near impossible to reach because she practically lived at the family bakery.

"Isn't this nice," I said, the chatter at Red's bar drowning out the awkward silence. I glared at Thad hoping he'd say something—start a conversation that didn't involve magic, blood, or dead people. Or cupcake orders.

"Yes." Thad raised his eyebrows. His skin was much more tanned than Junior's and his dark brown hair complemented the hickory shade of his eyes. "You know, I was just telling Ember about my new bike. Did you know it gets forty miles to the gallon?"

"I bet you would get fifty if you didn't drive like a maniac through town." Stevie brushed a lock of midnight hair from her shoulders. She'd been growing it out, and the longer length reminded me of how she'd looked in high school minus the sleeve of tattoos.

"Okay, then." I took a deep breath. "New topic. Did anyone see the paper today?"

"Oh, don't get me started on the *Misty Messenger*," Stevie commented. She studied the pile of hot wings, picking one out that met her standards. "It's gone down the toilet ever since Zinny left. That new editor, what's-her-name, has turned it into a gossip magazine. I mean, who cares about a stupid nip slip at the Pelican Playhouse? I care about *real* news."

Thad and Junior looked at each other.

"At least she's been reporting all the vandalism going on this summer," I added, trying to keep the conversation flowing. "Five times in one month. I think that's a first for Misty Key."

"Yeah well, she ruined everything the minute she named the vandal Boar Boy," Stevie argued. "Boar Boy strikes again." She waved her hands in the air. "Hey, if I wanted to read a comic book, I would have bought a comic book. Graffitiing Darlene's door is a misdemeanor, and she's glorifying a delinquent in the name of entertainment."

"Your passion for law intrigues me," Junior said. He'd shown up in a blue button-down. Even though he'd sold his family's law firm in Chattanooga, he still dressed like he was on his way to the office. He and Thad were like night and day, which was why they'd never gotten along that well. But vampires and shifters tended to clash anyway. Corpse Corp and Were & Company weren't exactly allies.

Stevie blushed.

Thad glanced up and nodded as a group of people entered the bar. More shifters. Misty Key was home to all sorts of magical species, including a clan of shifters that lived just outside city limits. They were of the canine variety, and they often ran free through the swamps at night. The residents of Misty Key didn't mind because all the non-magical folks were oblivious to the existence of magic.

My hometown had been a peaceful place my entire life.

"How about a round of drinks?" Junior said. "On me, of course."

His platinum hair shone like the sun as he headed toward the bar, weaving his way through the crowd.

"Man, it's crowded," I commented. "Is there a game or something I don't know about?"

"Will you ladies excuse me for a minute? My buddy Chetan over there owes me a twenty." Thad stood up, adjusting his T-shirt. It was hunter green just like the pair of hiking boots he used to wear when he'd first arrived in Misty Key—before he'd gotten a tad more acquainted with the humidity.

"No problem." I watched him walk away.

"Could you make it any more obvious?" Stevie muttered.

"What?"

"Oh, nothing." Stevie chuckled.

"So, I have a thing for Thad." I cleared my throat, directing my attention back at Stevie. "So what? This is nothing new."

"I still can't believe you convinced me to tag along on y'all's first date." She rubbed the sides of her arms. She'd chosen to wear one of her usual tank tops. It was practical for the daytime when the sun was out and the heat made the sidewalks sizzle like frying pans. But she'd forgotten that a lot of places, restaurants especially, compensated by blasting the AC.

"Junior has been trying to ask you out for months," I responded. "You two needed a helping hand."

"I'm not sure it was much help." Stevie lowered her voice, glancing over her shoulder. "I'm really bad at this. I doubt Junior will be calling me up for another date. Whoever heard of a psychic and a vampire hitting it off anyway?"

"You're doing great." I smiled wide, but Stevie wasn't buying it. She flashed me one of her usual stares. It gave me goosebumps.

"Don't lie to me. You know how much I hate liars."

"You just need to loosen up a little," I suggested. "Try not to talk about work or dead people."

"In other words, *don't* be myself," she replied.

"Uh . . ." I took a deep breath.

"You know what, it's too soon." She stood up, pushing in her chair. "I knew it was too soon for this sort of thing."

"No, it's not too soon." I grabbed her wrist and urged her to sit back down.

It had been over a month since she'd come clean about the father of her son—my ten-year-old nephew, Orion. Stevie had kept the truth a secret for far too long, and I didn't blame her. Thanks to a bogus spell bought off the shadow network, Orion's father was what was referred to as the living dead. For over ten years, Nate hadn't known he'd fathered a son. Until Lady Deja made a special trip to Lunar Bakery and found him thanks to her crystal ball.

Stevie had swallowed her pride and done one of the hardest things she might ever have to do.

She'd sent him a letter.

But she hadn't received a reply.

"I think I'm just destined to be alone," she muttered. "But I'm okay with that. I have Mom. I have Orion. I have Yogi and the bakery. I have plenty of stuff going on in my life."

"Stevie, just let yourself move on." I forced her to sit down again. "You and Junior have a lot in common. For starters, neither of you are freaked out by dead people."

"I talk to the dead, and he drinks the blood of corpses," she stated. "There's a big difference."

"Give him a chance," I insisted.

Junior returned to the table with drinks, and Stevie forced a fake smile. It was better than nothing. I knew it would take time to ease her into dating again and Junior knew all about Seers and the work we took on to help keep the peace among magical communities. He was the perfect fit.

As I casually searched the bar for Thad, a light flashed at me through the corner of my eye. It was a number. I tried to ignore it. I'd been working on controlling my psychic gift, turning it on and off whenever I had the chance. The more I learned to control it, the more my gift expanded and progressed into other areas of the six clairs.

"I grabbed us menus." Junior set a paper down in front of me, and another number jumped off the page.

It was a four.

My chest went tight.

Nothing good ever happened when I saw fours.

I hated fours.

My eyes darted around the bar. I studied every couple at every table until my gaze rested on Thad and his friend Chetan. Chetan was wearing a flannel shirt, and he appeared to be with someone. Thad and I locked eyes. I turned away, composing myself as he returned to our table.

"Sorry about that." Thad grabbed the nearest drink and took a swig.

"So, should we order more food? I hear their chocolate bread pudding is to die for." I clasped my hands together and rested them gently on the table.

Someone shouted, and the bar suddenly went quiet.

All the muscles in my body tensed, the noise piercing my chest. The numbers I'd seen ran through my mind and I was terrified of turning around, afraid of what I might see. Someone shouted again and I jumped, spilling my drink down my blouse.

"Yikes," Thad muttered, but he wasn't looking at me as he handed me a wad of napkins.

"What?" My eyes went wide.

"Chetan's date just dumped something down his shirt," Thad explained. "Bummer."

"Chocolate bread pudding," Stevie commented. "Yeah. He's going to need a good stain remover to get that out."

I finally turned around just as Thad's friend Chetan marched toward the bathrooms. The woman he'd walked in with immediately stormed outside. I took a deep breath. I could deal with a lovers' quarrel. It was far better than lots of other things numbers had tried to warn me about.

"Oh," I breathed. "Thank the cosmos."

Stevie eyed me suspiciously. "Care to share?"

"It's nothing," I responded. "Not a big deal."

I rubbed the stain on my blouse. My efforts to clean it were only making it worse. I gulped, feeling the heat of Thad's stare. We'd been through a lot together but for some reason, I was still a nervous wreck when he came around. Labeling our outing as our first official date wasn't helping.

"Why don't you let me help you with that?" Stevie's eyes went wide, and she tilted her head toward the restrooms.

"Uh, okay."

"Yeah. Wouldn't want it to stain." Stevie grabbed my hand and pulled me through the crowded room.

I was relieved when we left the chatter from the bar behind. The hallway next to the kitchen was much quieter. I took a deep breath, second-guessing my decision to turn my evening with Thad into a double date with my neighbor and older sister. I glanced up at the ceiling trying to calm my buzzing brain.

"Maybe Red's wasn't the best choice," I said.

I looked at Stevie and stopped.

Stevie wasn't paying attention.

She was too busy staring at the body lying face down on the tile floor.

"He's dead." Stevie gulped.

"No. No. No." I rubbed my eyes over and over again. "He can't be. I saw the numbers and then . . . the yelling. No. No, he can't be dead."

More and more numbers swirled through my head. I tried to turn them off but I couldn't. The numbers and patterns that made up the universe had a mind of their own. I just interpreted them. A bead of sweat formed on my cheek. If the man in front of me was dead that meant I was in for more trouble I didn't need.

"Sorry, Ember. He's dead."

"No." I shook my head, desperate for it not to be true. "I mean, are you sure? Check his pulse."

"I'm sure," Stevie insisted. "His ghost is practically telling me off as we speak. So rude. Even in the afterlife." My sister Stevie was a medium. She communicated with the dead and not all of them were friendly. I didn't know how she coped seeing dead people everywhere she went. But it explained why she was crabby most of the time.

"What's he saying?"

"He says he knows who killed him." Stevie's eyes went wide.

"Who?"

"Boar Boy."

Chapter 2

We waited outside Red's to be questioned.

"Who would want to hurt Chetan? Uncle Louie is going to be devastated." Thad crossed his arms, the starlight highlighting his sharp facial features. He glanced at a group of shifters standing right next to us.

My stomach churned, and the guilt hit me. It always did when I wasn't able to save someone from a terrible fate. I bit the side of my lip. I needed a moment alone with Stevie. She hadn't had the chance to explain the things Chetan had told her and I didn't know if his ghost was still hanging around the bar.

"I'm sorry, Thad."

"Yeah," Junior added. "And I'm sorry you two had to find him."

"Me too." Stevie stared down at the sidewalk.

Thad sniffed the air, and his eyes wandered around the crowded road in front of Red's bar. He'd told me once that he sensed things the way an animal did. I'd never really been sure what he'd meant by that. If he sensed my fears, he was too polite to say anything.

"Stevie, you're awfully quiet," Thad pointed out.

"So?" She shrugged.

"So, I can't help but ask," he continued. "Chetan was part of my pack. He was like a brother to me. Do you have any idea how he died?"

Stevie looked at me. "Thad—"

"I knew it," he said, raising his voice. "I knew Chetan wouldn't miss the chance to rat out his killer. You saw his ghost, didn't you?"

"Yes," Stevie muttered. "But I don't think *here* is the best place to talk about it." She glanced over her shoulder at the cop cars parked along the street.

"Just tell me what he told you," Thad insisted. "He couldn't have died of natural causes. He was perfectly healthy." He glanced over his shoulder at the group of shifters who seemed just as distraught. Stevie's ability to see the dead wasn't widely known in the magical community. But Thad knew.

"Well, you can never be too sure of that," Junior said.

Thad cleared his throat, ignoring Junior's comment. "Louie will push for an official investigation anyway, which means that a Seer will eventually be assigned to this case."

"Every time we go down this road, someone gets hurt," Stevie said. "Last time we almost lost the family bakery."

"Please." Thad pressed his hands together. "Please, help me, Stevie."

Thad turned to me next, and I couldn't disappoint him.

"He does have a point," I said. "Chetan was a shifter, and we both know that Louie won't stop until he gets answers. Just tell him."

Stevie rolled her eyes.

"Fine." She lowered her voice. "Promise me you won't go wolfman on everyone until we get some more details."

"Wolfman?" Thad wrinkled his nose. "What does that even mean?"

"I think she's referring to your doglike tendencies," Junior commented.

"You mean like ripping things apart with my bare teeth." He instinctually puffed out his chest.

Junior smirked. "Or playing fetch."

"I'll give you something to fetch, Junior." Thad took a step forward, and Junior took a step back.

"You two are impossible." I intervened before the insults turned into a fist fight. "What Stevie means is she doesn't want you causing a riot with the shifters before we know all the facts."

"In a nice way, yeah." Stevie kept a straight face as an officer walked past us. I didn't know how long we would be waiting before we were allowed to leave. At least it wasn't cold outside.

"Come on, Stevie. When have you ever known me to lose my cool?"

The few times I'd witnessed Thad shift from man to wolf flashed through my mind. The first had been terrifying to watch, but I was getting more and more used to it. Last time he'd shifted, he'd smelled like fishy swamp water. Next time I planned on offering to scrub him down with some of Yogi's vanilla-almond-scented doggy shampoo.

"Uh, when the moon is full," Junior said.

Thad clenched his jaw.

"I spoke with Chetan's ghost minutes after he died. He was really upset and said some things that didn't make sense." Stevie took a deep breath, observing the other people waiting on the sidewalk.

"Maybe I can make sense of it," Thad responded. "What did he say?"

Stevie cleared her throat. "He said it was Boar Boy."

Thad wrinkled his nose. "Boar Boy? You mean the guy the *Misty Messenger* won't shut up about?"

"That's the one."

"The graffiti artist?" Thad scratched the scruff on his chin. "No. That can't be right. No one knows who Boar Boy is. The police don't even know that."

"Evening, folks." Our conversation was interrupted by a familiar face.

"Detective," I replied.

The townsfolk liked to joke that Detective Winter had a heart made of ice that matched his ice blue eyes. Most of the time, I believed it. He never budged when it came to the fine print of the law, with the exception of the town's annual craft fair to raise money for charity. The detective had a hard exterior with surprising bits of sugar underneath.

"If it isn't the Greene sisters," he stated. "I should designate a private room for you two at the station. I'll get my best officer to decorate it too."

"That won't be necessary," Stevie chimed in. "We don't know anything."

"But you did find the body." He made a note in his phone.

"We happened to see it first," Stevie explained, impatiently tapping her foot. She distrusted cops as much as she did witches. "It was a busy hallway. Anyone could have found him."

"But *you* found him," the detective reiterated. His stern stature didn't waver, and Stevie was careful not to give away too much. Detective Winter was clueless when it came to magic, and the oath we took when obtaining our Seer license forbade us from revealing the existence of magic to humans unless it was life or death. Or the human figured it out all on her own and confronted you about it, which had been the case with my childhood friend Rickiah Pepper. She was my only non-magical friend who knew I had a psychic gift.

"Yes, we did." I nodded, hoping he'd leave once we told him everything we'd seen. For me, that wasn't much.

"And what were you doing in the hallway?"

I glanced down at the stain on my blouse. I hadn't gotten the chance to clean it properly before it left a mark.

"My sister and I were on our way to the bathroom," I explained. "I spilled something on my shirt."

"And you needed two of you to do that?" he asked, looking from me to Stevie.

"We're women. We go to the ladies' room in hordes." Stevie raised her eyebrows. Nothing could keep her from sarcasm. Not even possible jail time.

The detective glanced down at his phone again. "Did you notice anything near the body?"

"Not a thing," Stevie answered. "Not even blood."

"And she doesn't mean that in a disappointed sort of way," Junior added. "Just for the record, these ladies were with us all evening. Several witnesses can vouch for them."

"I'll get to you in a minute, Mr. Larson," the detective said. "Did you ladies witness an argument between the victim and a woman at the bar?"

"She dumped chocolate bread pudding all down his shirt," Stevie answered. "I'll bet it was piping hot."

"Do you know the woman?"

Stevie shook her head. "No. I can't say I do."

I hadn't recognized the woman either.

"I know her." Thad spoke up. "Her name is Athena Davis. She's in town visiting family."

Davis. That last name sounded familiar.

Davis. The family of sirens.

I crossed my arms, avoiding making eye contact with Stevie. She wasn't going to like what I had to say. A siren had a spat with a shifter, and now a shifter was dead. This was going to cause a whole lot of trouble.

More trouble than I wanted to admit.

19

Chapter 3

"I liked you better as a cat."

Stevie filled the display cases with pastries as I sat at an empty table with my morning coffee. The family bloodhound, Yogi, sat by my feet. Stevie's baking assistant, Ike, wiped the front counter while retelling one of his usual stories about the silver mines he'd worked in. Being born in 1877, miners, gunfights, and rhubarb pie were all he talked about. And then there was his not-so-secret crush on Luann.

"No one listened to me when I was a cat," Ike responded. "Anyway, my pal Lyle's pistol fell right down the well and—"

"Okay, I'm going to have to cut you off." Stevie held up her hands. "We have a busy morning ahead of us, and I still haven't finished icing the Good Vibes Vanilla cakes."

"Oh, let Whiskers talk." My little sister Aqua entered the room carrying a tray of chocolate croissants. They were her favorite item on the menu.

"It's *Ike*," Stevie snapped. "Because every time you call him Whiskers, customers ask how he got that nickname and then Luann blabs to the whole world that Ike was cursed by a witch in the 1800s and used to be a black cat named Whiskers. And at the same time, all of us fumble around telling lies to cover up the truth and trying to get her to shut up. We talked about this, remember?"

"That only happened once." Aqua tugged her braids that showed off her latest hair care project—turquoise streaks. She liked it when her hair matched her name.

"Once was enough," Stevie said. "There are enough rumors going around town these days thanks to the *Misty Messenger*. I want no part of it."

"Fine." Aqua set down her tray and crossed her arms. "I won't call Ike Whiskers during business hours."

"How about at all?" Stevie raised her eyebrows. She thrived on confrontation, and she and Aqua had been known to bicker like an old married couple for hours if no one stopped them.

"I don't mind being called Whiskers," Ike chimed in, rubbing his button nose. He was petite but still strong enough to chop up a wheelbarrow of firewood, which he'd done on his first day before learning how modern-day appliances worked.

"Ike, stay out of this."

"Don't talk to Ike like that." Aqua placed a hand on his round shoulder. "He's practically family. You're just mad because your date with Junior last night didn't go so well."

Stevie glared at me.

I knew better than to tell Aqua anything when it came to relationships. She just couldn't keep her mouth shut.

"I didn't say anything."

"It's true. She didn't. I read it in the *Misty Messenger*."

"The *Misty Messenger* is reporting on my dating life?" Stevie's nostrils flared. "If that's true then another crime is about to be committed around here."

"You promised me I could make my famous whistle berries tonight," Ike complained.

"She's not serious," I explained. "It's just an expression."

Aqua gestured toward Stevie. "Ike, this is what we refer to nowadays as a nervous breakdown. It's when someone loses their mind for no apparent reason."

"Shush, Aqua."

"And the papers don't care about your dating life," Aqua continued. "That would be the most boring column in the world. The dead guy at Red's was on the front page this morning."

"What did the article say?" I narrowed my eyes.

"Something about a fight he had with some girl and then he dropped dead." Aqua snagged a chocolate croissant. Her first one of the day.

I shook my head. "The local paper is just going to make the situation worse."

"Wait until Louie reads that," Stevie commented. "The shifters are going to riot in the streets if justice isn't served."

"We don't know that for sure." I stared down at my coffee as Yogi perked his head up.

There was a knock on the front door despite the fact that our hours were posted outside. We didn't open for another thirty minutes. Our other bakery employee, Luann, wasn't due to arrive for another fifteen.

Yogi sniffed the air and trotted to the door.

A knock sounded through the café again.

"I'll get it," Aqua said.

"No, you need to go back into the kitchen and start some more vanilla buttercream," Stevie instructed. "And check on those sourdough loaves. They should be done in a couple of minutes."

"I'll get it," I volunteered, rushing to the front entrance while Stevie and Ike continued with their morning tasks.

Yogi let out a soft bark as I opened the door and saw Nova, our regional representative. Yogi sniffed the air again before retreating to my office back behind the kitchen. Yogi wasn't fond of the Siamese cat that trailed behind Nova everywhere she went. Well, *ghost* cat. The only ones annoyed by its presence were Stevie and Yogi.

"I thought I'd stop by before you're too busy to talk." Nova walked straight into the bakery and sat down at her usual table in the corner. She looked up, admiring the peach-colored walls and the gold constellations my mom had painted on the ceiling when the bakery first opened. I never tired of looking at them either.

"This is about last night, isn't it?" I sat down across from her. Chetan's case was sure to be extremely time consuming, and Stevie was already on edge. More so than usual.

"Last night? No, I'm here about the letter you received in the mail." Nova wrinkled her nose and gently smoothed the sides of her auburn bun. She wore cat-shaped stud earrings and a matching charm bracelet.

"The stress thing?"

"Uh-huh." Nova's purse hit the table with a loud thud. She dug through it, pulling out a bright yellow folder.

Stevie joined us at the table, setting a teacup and orange roll in front of Nova.

"I don't want to hear anything about my energy alignment or clogged chakras," Stevie stated. "Just eat the pastry."

Nova's psychic talent was something called clairgustance—one of the six clairs. It was the ability to interpret people by using food as a vessel. It was a gift that set her up for lots of awkward dinner parties, especially when she made comments about the pot roast tasting like infidelity. It was a complicated talent I was glad I didn't own. I would have hated trying to turn it on and off just to be able to enjoy a nice meal.

"Nice to see you, Stevie." Nova handed the two of us packets titled *How to Manage Your Stress: A Guide for Beginners*.

"Is this a joke?" Stevie flipped through it.

"No." Nova shook her head. "Taking on Seer responsibilities is stressful work, and Lady Deja wants to make sure y'all are managing your stress to the best of your ability."

"This is about Trace's heart attack, isn't it?" Stevie raised her eyebrows. We'd gotten to know some of the other Seers in our region on a recent psychic retreat. We'd since all tried to keep in touch.

"His little incident might have contributed to this, yes," she admitted.

24

"I think it was all the red meat and butter that contributed to it," Stevie added.

Nova lifted her chin. She was used to resistance from Stevie. No matter how hard she tried to steer the conversation in a positive manner, Stevie always found things to complain about. Some days were better than others, but either way, Nova didn't seem to mind.

"I am here to invite you both to participate in Lady Deja's Stress Management Challenge," she explained. "You will see here on the first page of your packets an explanation about stress and how it can impact your everyday life."

"'Side effects of living in a stressful environment include irritability, mood swings, and insomnia,'" I recited, trying not to stare at Stevie. "Sounds familiar."

"On the next page are all kinds of tasks you can do to help reduce and relieve stress in your life," Nova went on. "Each task has been assigned points. Points will be tallied in one month's time, and each region will announce a winner."

"What's the prize?" Stevie crossed her arms, checking the time.

"Always right to the point, aren't we." Nova took a tiny sip of her coffee. "The winners will receive a private reading from Lady Deja and a cash prize of one thousand dollars."

"One thousand dollars?" Stevie squinted at the list, skimming each item. "So, if I do all these things I'll win one thousand dollars?"

"There are one hundred things on that list," she responded. "I doubt you'll have time to complete every single task. It's all about the points added up at the end. And points for each task will only be awarded once. You can't just do one thing over and over again and expect to win."

"We have to earn as many points as we can in a limited amount of time?" I said. "Isn't that a little stressful?" I bit the side of my lip. I couldn't help pointing out the irony.

"Light a candle," Stevie read aloud. "Take a bubble bath. Sleep an extra hour. I don't have time for all this."

"Item forty-seven," I stated. "Replace one negative comment with one positive one every day for ten days."

"Doing something like that will stress me out even more," Stevie muttered.

"I'm just the messenger." Nova took one last sip of coffee before standing up to leave. "All licensed Seers have the option to participate. That doesn't mean you have to do it, though."

"So Aqua is out. Less competition." Stevie nodded.

My little sister, Aqua, had found out during her crest reading that she was able to communicate with animals. She was a pet psychic. The first in our family. But she was still studying for her license.

"We could use new accounting software," I said, thinking out loud. "I've had my eye on a program I've been wanting to try for a couple of months now."

"Uh, I don't think so," Stevie argued. "We need a new mixer. Have you seen Ike around the appliances? I'm surprised our ovens still work."

"If I win, the prize money will be mine to spend," I pointed out.

Nova looked from me to Stevie.

"I'd better get going." She secured her purse and headed for the exit. Ike greeted her by tipping his imaginary hat and opening the door.

"We don't have time for this," Stevie stated as soon as Nova was gone. "Do we?"

I glanced down at the list. Each item was meant to both help us relax a little and not let the stress of daily life make us sick. Yes, the money was nice, and the reading from Lady Deja was priceless, but I'd already lost a loved one to heart disease. Not Trace. My father.

Stevie possessed some of his overly anxious qualities. She also had a son who depended on her and a bakery that thrived because she was a gifted baker unlike me. But I knew she wouldn't go for it unless she had something to prove.

"I do," I stated. "And I'm going to win that money and spend it all on computer software."

"Not if I have anything to say about it." She forced a smile and glanced at the packet. "Or *not*. Instead of telling you how ridiculous you sound, I'm choosing to compliment Ike on his sweeping skills."

"Well, thank you, Miss Stevie." Ike smiled and nodded.

Stevie pretended to check an item off her list. "This is going to be easy."

I watched her strut into the kitchen to finish icing her cakes.

"If Stevie asks," I said to Ike, "I'm . . ." I skimmed the list looking for tasks with the most points. ". . . I'm

27

meditating every morning and . . . training for a 5K race. Got it?"

"Okay." Ike looked a little confused. "Are you actually going to do those things?"

"What matters is that Stevie gives this stress relief stuff a try," I explained. "She will because she doesn't like to lose."

"Aqua always tells me I don't understand women." Ike touched his chin, uttering the words to himself like I wasn't even in the room. "This must be what she meant because I have no idea what Ember's talking about."

"Uh, Ike?"

He turned and looked at me. "Oh, sorry. When I was a cat the only person I really talked to was myself. Old habit."

He cleared his throat and skipped into the kitchen. It was like a breath of fresh air having him around. Stevie's comments and complaints didn't seem to get to him. I think it was mostly because he didn't understand them. But still, I hoped he would stick around for a while. I wanted Stevie to stick around for a while too. I couldn't imagine how often her blood pressure spiked throughout the day.

The stress challenge was step one.

Step two was convincing her to take a day off once a week.

And step three was getting back the calm and happy Stevie I knew was in there somewhere.

Chapter 4

Stevie smiled like an evil genius.

"I'm normally good at this online." Zinny Pellman made a face as she pushed her poker chips toward Stevie. She grabbed another one of Stevie's sugar-free brownies and took a giant bite.

"Retirement has made you soft," Stevie responded.

I sat next to Stevie in a room in the back of Darlene Johnston's antiques shop. It was poker night, an occasion Stevie had never missed since accepting an invitation to join the club, and all of the usual participants were present. Darlene smiled, adjusting her bright green visor. She'd claimed it was her lucky visor that had helped her win two hundred dollars in Vegas one summer.

"Or maybe it's all the drinking," Mary Jean commented. Despite her conservative views and regular church attendance, she still showed up for Darlene's poker games. But she was never without a snide comment about giving in to the devil's vices.

"Thanks, Mary Jean, but I think I just need to find a new hobby." Zinny huffed as she brushed a strand of silvery hair from her face.

"Write a book," Darlene suggested, shuffling the cards.

"I think I'm done writing for a while," Zinny answered. "The *Misty Messenger* burned me out, or maybe it's the diabetes." She took another bite of Stevie's homemade brownie.

"Well, I have to say I find the paper much more informative these days." Mary Jean glanced down at the bible verse on her oversized T-shirt.

I clenched my jaw, knowing how much Stevie loathed the *Misty Messenger* since it had been rebranded by an out-of-towner.

"What? Are you serious?" Stevie glared at Mary Jean. "The stuff they print isn't news. Tell her, Zinny. That stuff isn't news."

"Hey, last time I checked they were broke, and now they're not," Zinny said. "They're going to print whatever sells."

"I don't want to read about who's dating who and the latest celebrity sighting at the Crystal Grande Hotel," Stevie went on. "We get enough of that crap from TV."

"I, for one, am glad that they published that article about the scandalous production at the Pelican Playhouse," Mary Jean stated. "Now I won't be wasting my money on a ticket. And what about that horrible display at Red's? Now everyone in town will finally understand that bars are bad news."

"Wait a minute." I waved my hands. "We don't know what really happened at Red's last night. Let's not jump to conclusions."

"I read all about the bar fight," Mary Jean continued. "It was an obvious lovers' spat that led to mortal sin thanks to the contribution of too much alcohol."

"So, you won't be wanting your usual glass of red after round five?" Darlene chuckled as she passed out the cards.

Zinny laughed as she looked at her hand. "Mary Jean a sinner?"

"At least my butt is on a pew every Sunday," she muttered, rearranging her hand. "That's more than I can say about you."

"Sunday is my rest day." Zinny cleared her throat and placed her cards face down on the table. "And I have a confession to make."

The four of us fell silent.

"The brownies are no good?" Stevie guessed. "I debated whether or not to use peanut butter."

"No, the brownies are great," she said. "I know y'all are apprehensive about the changes being made at the *Misty Messenger* so I invited a special guest to our game. But she's late."

"Oh no you didn't." Stevie's eyes went wide.

"I did." Zinny took a deep breath. "Look, the *Misty Messenger* was my life for so long, and I couldn't imagine this town without it. And then some younger folks came along and kept it going. I'm not there anymore, but the paper will always have a little piece of my heart. Y'all should accept the fact that change happens. It doesn't have to be a bad thing."

Stevie bit the side her lip.

I nodded. Zinny did have a point. The local paper's new angle didn't bother me as much as it bothered Stevie. But that was because I'd avoided reading it for years and now it was just habit not to pay it any attention. I waited for Stevie to say something.

"Okay." Darlene nodded. "Hey, the more the merrier. My grandkids are coming for a visit next week, and I can use all the cash I can get."

"I second that." Stevie lifted her chin. "Let's clean her out when she gets here."

"That's the spirit." Zinny finally smiled, but I knew it would be easier said than done.

The five of us played another round. I ended up folding before volunteering to grab another bag of chips from Darlene's office. I slowly walked through the front of Darlene's darkened antiques shop, avoiding the shelves of porcelain dolls that always seemed to be staring at me.

Darlene's office was crowded with boxes of flea market finds. I maneuvered through the mess to get to her grocery bag full of extra snacks. A noise right behind me made me jump. I clutched my chest as I turned around and saw Stevie. Her jaw was clenched and her hands were on her hips.

"Geez," I blurted out. "How many times do I have to tell you not to sneak up on me like that." I grabbed the bag of potato chips.

"Can you believe Zinny invited what's-her-face?"

"It explains the extra container of sour cream and onion dip," I said. "And you know her name. You're going to have to say it out loud eventually."

Stevie tapped her foot. "I know I'm just trying to blow off some steam before she gets here. Maybe this is for the best. I'll give her a piece of my mind and be done with it."

I narrowed my eyes.

That was a bad idea.

"No, you won't. You're going to play nice."

"Why?"

"Because we have mouths to feed and the last thing we need is an article in the paper about how we use expired milk or something dumb like that."

"We don't use expired anything."

"I know. The point is that you shouldn't make it your mission to piss off the new editor-in-chief. Got it?" I couldn't be sure that Stevie would agree. She was stubborn, and at the end of the day, I knew she'd do whatever she wanted anyway. But it didn't hurt to try.

Stevie glared in my direction—a concentrated stare I'd seen many times before. The face came naturally. It was her way of discerning the living from the dead, and I knew for a fact that the dead were all over Darlene's antiques shop. Most notably, Darlene's great-grandmother who wholeheartedly disapproved of poker night and didn't care who knew it.

"Is it the old lady again?" I followed Stevie's gaze, and it gave me goosebumps. "On second thought, I don't want to know about the ghosts eavesdropping on our conversation right now. I have a bag of chips to deliver."

"I think you should cheat," Stevie stated. "It would make me feel a lot better."

"Cheat?"

"You know what I mean."

My psychic talent extended to all the numbers and patterns that made up the universe, and when I could hone them, I could read just about anyone. Including a bunch of ladies sitting around a poker table. But cheating was against the oath I'd taken when I'd obtained my Seer license. I promised I would use my gifts to help others, not tear them down in the name of a selfish cause. It created a whole lot of bad karma in return.

"No way." I shook my head. "Get one of your ghost friends to do it for you."

"You're no fun." She stomped out of Darlene's office, joining me back at the table with more refreshments.

The five of us played another hand before our sixth player arrived.

Zinny's smile was genuine. She wrapped her arm around the *Misty Messenger's* new editor and introduced her to the group. My stomach churned as I waited for my sister's reaction. There was a fifty-fifty chance she would go on a rant about how gossip magazines were destroying the minds of our youth.

"Everyone, this is Tillie Hodge," Zinny announced. "Tillie, this is everyone."

"Nice to meet you, ladies." Tillie grinned—a scrunched smile that emphasized her tiny mouth. She wore jeans and a plain black T-shirt that contrasted with her ginger-blonde hair. It was long and wavy, and she looked like she'd just stepped out of the shower. She seemed harmless, but that didn't mean she wasn't.

"Thank you for inviting me," Tillie added.

"Of course, welcome to Misty Key." Darlene gestured toward an open seat. "Ever played Texas Hold'em?"

"I'm a little rusty, but I think I can get back in the groove." Tillie sat next to me. She looked to be about my age—mid-thirties. I scooted over as Darlene dealt the cards.

"Nice to meet you—"

"Ember Greene," I said, shaking her hand. "My sister and I"—I nodded toward Stevie—"own Lunar Bakery."

"Oh, I've seen that place," Tillie answered. "I need to try it sometime."

Stevie stayed silent. A rarity.

"The locals seem to like it," I added.

"I'm sure they do." Tillie carefully looked at her cards. "This is a tourist town but how often do the locals venture out of southern Alabama, am I right?"

"Where are you from, Tillie?" Darlene asked.

"Albuquerque," she replied. "Five bucks to anyone who can spell that." She chuckled.

"I'll spell something for ya," Stevie muttered.

Tillie was starting to put a sour taste in my mouth, but I tried to change the subject.

"So, you're used to the heat then?" I forced a smile.

"And decent Mexican food," she added. "If any of you know a place I would be happy to try it out. I do have to warn you, though. I'm a harsh critic when it comes to green chiles."

"Just green chiles?" Stevie kept her eyes on her cards.

35

"I'm sorry, what's your name?" Tillie looked right at Stevie.

The entire table watched Stevie like she was a firecracker about to explode.

"Stevie." She reached for Tillie's hand. "Short for Stevana."

"Interesting name," Tillie commented.

"I was named after my dad, Steven," she explained. "And if you want my advice, embrace the southernness of this place. The food included."

"I'll keep that in mind, Stevie."

I took a deep breath, hoping that was all Stevie had to say.

"Mary Jean," Mary Jean shouted from the end of the table. "So glad to have you here in Misty Key. I read your paper every morning."

"Well, thank you, Mary Jean."

"I have to say that I admire your dedication to reporting *everything* that goes on around here," Mary Jean went on. I rubbed my forehead. Mary Jean was picking at a scab that was best left untouched.

"That's my job." Tillie nodded proudly. "Leave no one in the dark. That's my motto."

"And I appreciated your commentary about the dangers of excessive drinking," Mary Jean said.

"Oh, you must be talking about the incident at Red's," Tillie said. "Scary stuff."

"And a one-time thing," I blurted out. "Misty Key is a very friendly place."

"I don't know." Tillie leaned back in her seat, crossing her arms. "I've seen some pretty disturbing police records that could affect the tourism around here if the information fell into the wrong hands. It seems your crime rate has increased over the past year."

"This is still one of the safest towns in all of Alabama." Stevie cleared her throat. "I should know. I grew up here, and I'm raising my son here too."

"Not according to what happened at Red's last night," Tillie argued.

My stomach churned some more. So much for Stevie's goal of avoiding negativity. With Tillie around, I feared her stress levels would shoot through the roof along with her blood pressure.

"No one knows what happened last night." Stevie hit her hand on the table. "What you published in the paper means nothing. It's just rumors. All of it. Rumors. Rumors. Rumors."

"I don't think so." Tillie smirked, pleased at the reaction she'd gotten out of Stevie. "A man was killed, and it could have been a heart attack, but it could have been murder."

Chapter 5

"I'm tearing it down."

The thought of *brunching* with a friend had never exhausted me until the day I'd had brunch with Elizabeth Carmichael. She was the owner of the Crystal Grande Hotel, and she'd hired me as a consultant to help her with hotel renovations. Mainly, she needed me to act as a voice of reason between her and the Misty Key Women's Society, who had protested Elizabeth's changes to begin with.

"What?" I set my teacup back down on the table. "Mrs. Carmichael, you can't just tear down the library. It was built over a hundred years ago."

"Don't call me Mrs.," she insisted. "My husband's dead, honey."

"Miss?"

"Elizabeth," she clarified. She dabbed the corner of her mouth with a napkin. Her acrylic nails were the same shade of lavender as her skirt. "You should let me finish before you butt in. I thought you went to business school."

"Go ahead and finish then."

"I'm tearing it down and rebuilding it," she explained, carefully selecting a cucumber sandwich. A tray of assorted finger foods had been placed in front of us. I avoided the miniature pastries. I got enough of them at home, and I knew Stevie would grill me about the taste and texture of the sweets baked in the Crystal Grande kitchen.

At least the Crystal Grande still ordered bread from us every week.

"Why? The library is gorgeous. It's one of the most iconic things about this place beside the private beach." My heart raced at the thought of a piece of the landmark being destroyed.

Memories of the hotel flashed through my mind. It sat on top of a hill above a white sandy beach, and it held countless family memories. As a child, I used to think of the hotel as a castle run by mermaids. The large plantation-style building had white columns and artistic balconies that made it look a magical place. I remembered the way the morning mist blended into the rolling waves when I'd delivered the weekly loaves of bread on my bicycle back in high school. I also remembered standing in the lobby with my dad—moments I'd clung to after he'd passed away.

"Fine. I have a hidden agenda. I'm sick of all the secrecy." She took a sip of tea. "My husband built a hidden passageway from our top floor suite to the main level of the hotel. What else did he hide from me? I won't be able to sleep easy until I know about every nook and cranny under my own roof."

"So, you're tearing down the wall to spite your dead husband?"

"It sounds silly when you put it that way," Elizabeth responded. "Think of it more as a discovery project. I mean if your house had hidden doorways and secret rooms, wouldn't you want to know?"

"Well, yeah." I shrugged. "I see your point, but the women's society won't be happy. You should choose your words very carefully."

"Those tacky society ladies." She rolled her eyes. "I thought I would never hear the end of if that time Jewel went into town in her bikini."

"*String bikini*," I added. "Yes, I remember. Those pictures were everywhere all summer long."

"Listen, the twins are adults now." She glanced around the dining room as guests were escorted to open tables. "I can't force them to behave accordingly. Lord knows I can't force Jewel to put some clothes on, but as long as the hotel is a trendy place, I can keep them away from Hollywood."

"How about this?" I paused, staring down at my teacup and hoping the right words would come to me. "Don't say you're tearing down the library. Instead, say you're rebuilding it to give more of a modern feel while still keeping its charming trademarks like the floor to ceiling bookshelves and collection of vintage furniture."

"I like it," she replied. "I'll put all those dusty books in a glass display case. The ladies can't argue with that."

"See. It's not that hard to compromise."

"I want you to feed the story to the local paper," Elizabeth added.

"What?" After what Stevie had said to Tillie during poker night, I wanted to keep my communication with her to a minimum. The anxiety bubbled around in my chest every time I thought of the next big headline.

"Yeah. My publicist is on maternity leave. I need someone to draft a story that makes me look good."

"Writing isn't my specialty," I said. "Numbers are my specialty."

"Words. Numbers." She snagged another cucumber sandwich and frowned. "If you're good with one, I'm sure you're good with the other. These sandwiches are too dry. I talked to Margaret about this last week. And where are the cruffins?"

Elizabeth raised her hand until a waitress eagerly approached our table.

"Okay." I took a deep breath. The paycheck was worth it, and the bakery needed all the extra cash flow it could get. "I guess I can invite the new editor at the *Misty Messenger* to some sort of groundbreaking. If you talk about the hotel's history, it'll make you seem less intimidating."

"I already started construction," she confessed. "Samantha, where are the cruffins? Our brunch trays are supposed to be hip and trendy, not filled with bland cucumber sandwiches."

"Sorry, ma'am," our waitress responded. "I'll go and ask."

"You do that." Elizabeth waved her hand again, and Samantha hurried into the kitchen. "You know, some days I love this place and some days I hate it. It's like visiting my parents in Birmingham."

A breeze swept through the dining room along with distant whispering. I looked toward the lobby and saw Jewel Carmichael headed for our table. Petite and blonde like her mother, she was much more attractive than her twin,

Jonathon, who took after the late George Carmichael, sporting stubby fingers and thick brows.

"I can't believe this." Jewel handed her mother her cell phone. "Look at that. Will you just look at that? Someone ought to have that woman fired." Jewel sat at our table, and it was the first time I'd seen her in person wearing something other than a swimsuit.

"Calm down, honey." Elizabeth's voice remained steady, her eyes darting briefly around the room at the other guests. "Stay and have some sweet tea. You know we're always being watched from the moment we leave our suites to the moment we're back upstairs for the evening."

"So you've said," Jewel answered. "Just about every day since I was twelve. Just read it."

Elizabeth squinted as she stared at her daughter's phone. "Geez. Where's the zoom on this?"

"You need to start carrying around your reading glasses, Mom."

"I don't need my glasses."

"Oh, just give it to me." Jewel snatched the phone back. "That new editor over at the *Misty Messenger* launched a blog, and I'm all over it. Seriously. She says I'm sneaking around with one of the pool boys."

"Not again, Jewel. I can't afford to fire another pool boy. There aren't enough vulnerable young men in this town who will work for minimum wage as it is."

"It's not true, Mother." Jewel rolled her eyes. "It's a gossip site just like all the others. Now nowhere is safe for me. Not even my own hotel."

"That little tart doesn't know who she's dealing with," Elizabeth muttered. "This isn't *Real Housewives of Misty Key*."

"Ew. Mom, you promised you would stop bringing up the marriage thing." Jewel twirled a strand of hair, keeping a smile on her face as she complained. After a minute of flipping through her phone some more, Jewel finally noticed there was someone else sitting at the table. "Uh, who is she?"

"I'm Ember," I answered.

"She's with me," Elizabeth added.

"Oh. Do I know you?" Jewel looked me up and down. Her pink sundress was much fancier than my casual work wear—tan slacks and a white blouse. Stevie had made fun of it before I'd left the house, saying I resembled burnt toast.

"No," I replied.

"You must be new in town." Jewel nodded.

"I grew up in Misty Key." I bit the inside of my cheek to stop myself from saying anything else.

"Ember, do you know this woman at the paper?" Elizabeth crossed her arms, making a similar facial expression as her daughter.

"I met her once." And once had been enough.

"Is she well liked?" Elizabeth paused, waiting for my answer.

"That depends on who you ask." It was the most diplomatic thing I could think to say.

43

"Well, she's new in town. I'll have my assistant invite her to brunch. That'll scare the confidence out of her."

"I just want my face off of her website." Jewel lifted her chin. "This is like the peach festival in Marietta all over again." She stood and marched back into the lobby.

"Poor girl." Elizabeth lowered her voice. "It's not easy being a Carmichael, you know."

"I will take your word for it."

"Scratch the newspaper article," she responded. "I'll handle the *Misty Messenger.* You just make sure those society ladies don't start another petition. I can only sweet-talk the mayor so many times. That man is handsy."

"Keeping the old and dusty books will help your cause," I pointed out.

"And in the meantime, if my husband has more skeletons in his closet, I'm going to find them."

Chapter 6

Yogi barked.

"Stop feeding him under the table," Stevie complained. "Yogi already has a problem with begging as it is."

"Granny, I've decided what I'm going to say on my first day of school," Orion replied, sneaking the family dog another handful of my mom's sweet chicken salad.

"Go ahead then, sweetie." My mom smiled, urging her grandson to continue.

Orion stood and took a deep breath. His hair was the same shade of black as Stevie's, but his eyes were an ocean blue I'd always guessed belonged to his father. He cleared his throat, staring at the kitchen sink.

"This summer I went to the beach, helped my mom at the bakery, and went to the dump with Auntie Aqua where a man gave us a free box of pizza."

"You promised you wouldn't tell anyone about that," Aqua muttered from across the table.

"You fed my son food from the city dump?" Stevie gripped her fork a little tighter. Yogi stayed under the table, and my mom tugged at the moonstone she wore around her neck. The running joke was that she planned on leaving it to her favorite daughter when she died. At the moment, Aqua was not the favorite.

"Relax, it was only a week past the expiration date. Frozen pizza lasts for months."

"The dump was awesome," Orion continued. "I think I saw a rat."

"Deep breaths, sweetie," my mom intervened. She dished Stevie up another helping of sweet chicken salad. It was my mom's specialty, and it went great with the day-old bread from the bakery.

"You guys are starting to freak out Yogi," Aqua pointed out, glancing under the table.

"Maybe I'll light a candle," Stevie replied, her mouth oozing with sarcasm. "That'll make all of these angry feelings go away."

"Yes, do that." Aqua kept a smile on her face.

"You took my son to the dump and basically fed him garbage," she argued. Her cheeks went rosy. "What is the matter with you? Sometimes I wonder how you even got a high school diploma in the first place."

"Must have been the same idiot who let you pass culinary school."

"Okay." My mom hit her hand on the table, her chestnut eyes as wide as donut holes. "You two better stop it, or one of you is painting the front door gray."

"Not me. I like the lemon yellow. It puts me in a good mood." Aqua quietly played with her braid.

"Fine." Stevie inhaled a little too loudly. "At least my son is still alive."

"See, there's a bright side to everything." My mom grabbed a packet of papers from the kitchen counter.

"Stevie, you had a rough day. Why don't you draw yourself a nice bubble bath?"

"Are you referring to item thirty-two on the list?" I asked.

"Oh, not that stress list," Stevie said.

"It's an *anti*-stress list," I corrected her. "And it won't hurt to give it a try."

"I'll take a bath when you start exercising." She took a bite of her sandwich.

"Good one, Mom. There's no way Auntie Ember will ever do that." Orion ripped his bread into tiny pieces, one of his many tactics to get out of eating everything on his plate.

"Now, what is that supposed to mean?" I wrinkled my nose. "Sure I've been slacking lately in that department, but I lived in New York City for a long time. I walked everywhere."

"Mom says if you don't move it, you don't lose it." Orion nodded matter-of-factly.

"Well, thank you for your honesty," I replied. "It's nice to know I'm the topic of conversation before bed every night."

"Oh, no. Before bed, Mommy talks about her hair and the size of vampire's fangs."

Aqua covered her mouth to hold back laughter.

"Orion, hon, I think it's time you went upstairs to get ready for bed."

"What?" he whined.

"Go on." Stevie tilted her head toward the staircase. "Take Yogi with you."

"Vampire fangs, huh?" I crossed my arms. "So, you did have a good time with Junior before it all went downhill."

"I thought we were talking about stress relief. I don't feel relieved of my stress right now." Stevie was quick to change the subject.

"Let me see that paper." Aqua grabbed my mom's copy. "Wow. I would win this challenge in a heartbeat, and then I'd ask Lady Deja for all the deets on my future husband."

"You're not eligible, sissy." Stevie pushed aside her dinner plate.

"Look at this one," Aqua continued. "You get fifty points for participating in an official athletic event. That's the one I would do. The Crawdaddy 5K is next weekend."

"How is running supposed to relieve stress?" Stevie asked. "Just thinking about it makes me the opposite of calm."

"You're up before the sun anyway," Aqua pointed out. "I'm sure Junior would be impressed."

"I don't care what Junior thinks." Stevie narrowed her eyes.

I stood up and held my mom's vanilla candle in my hand. She had candles all around the house, and she lit them often, saying that the calming aromas promoted peace in the home. I searched the nearest drawer for a lighter and lit the candle. I took a whiff of the vanilla scent and placed it on the counter.

"That's one point for me," I said.

"What are you doing?" Stevie paused, studying the flame as it swayed from side to side.

"I'm earning points." I shrugged. It had come to my attention that my entire family needed a breather, not just Stevie. It had been an emotional roller coaster for all of us after my dad had passed away. My mom had taken a step back from work, Stevie had taken over the family business, and I'd taken a finance job in New York City. But now I was back in my hometown sharing Stevie's load, and none of us had fully adjusted to the new dynamic.

I just hoped I was helping.

"So, you were serious. You're going to try and win the grand prize."

"Yeah." I nodded, knowing the extra effort would only add to my daily to-do list, but I was willing to give it a try if it meant that Stevie would relax once in a while.

"Then I guess I'll see you two bright and early in the morning," Aqua joked. "Y'all can go running with me. That is, if you two can keep up."

"Don't even start with me," Stevie chimed in. "I'm good at sports when I feel like making an effort."

"Sure." Aqua twirled a turquoise curl around her finger and cautiously headed upstairs.

"I hate it when you girls argue," my mom muttered. She touched her moonstone. It hung from her neck on a dainty silver chain that sparkled underneath the light in the kitchen. "You know, when I'm gone all y'all will have is each other."

"Yes, we know," Stevie said. "And your magical moonstone will be left to your favorite daughter."

"Or favorite grandson," she added. "I still haven't decided." She took a sip of sweet tea and stood to clear the table. Her T-shirt was baggier than usual. There were days I had to remind her to eat something and those days seemed to be frequent.

"Mom, sit down. I'll take care of the dishes." I took her plate, and Stevie followed my lead.

"Ember may suck at baking, but she doesn't suck at dishwashing," Stevie responded.

"Oh, be nice, Stevie." My mom chuckled.

"Yeah, be nice," I added. "You've never tried my signature breakfast."

"Is it a microwaved egg?" Stevie laughed at her own joke.

I took a moment to formulate a good comeback, but a knock at the front door pulled me from my thoughts. Yogi barked as he ran down the stairs. I looked at Stevie and she shrugged.

"Well, I'm not expecting anyone," my mom said.

I wiped my hands on my blouse and hurried to the front door. Yogi stayed by my side wagging his tail. My heart raced when I opened the door and saw Thad. I waited for his usual grin, but his expression was nervous. He glanced over his shoulder, stepping into the living room before I'd even invited him inside.

Yogi wagged his tail even more and licked Thad's knuckles. The two of them had a special canine bond that Aqua liked to tease him about. Thad took a deep breath and paced in front of the couch before explaining why he'd shown up on my doorstep. Stevie and my mom entered the living room, and I saw Aqua poke her head into the upstairs hallway to listen in.

"Thad, quit freaking us out," Stevie finally said. "Why are you here and why do you look like you're ready to blow your groceries?"

"If he barfs, can I see it?" Orion shouted from the top of the stairs.

"No." Stevie frowned. "Go get ready for bed and don't make me tell you again."

"Okay." Orion exhaled loudly, stomping back to his room.

"I'm sorry to show up like this," Thad said, running his fingers through his dark, shaggy hair. "I didn't know what else to do." His eyes darted from one corner of the room to the other.

I gulped. "This is about Chetan, isn't it?"

Thad nodded.

"That article in the *Misty Messenger* caused an uproar," Thad explained. "Because Athena Davis is a siren, some of the other shifters think the sirens should be forced to leave Misty Key."

"Surely Louie has this under control," my mom cut in.

"Louie sent me here." Thad's gaze finally rested on Stevie. "He sent me here for you, Stevie. He wants you to contact Chetan's spirit so he can clear everything up."

"But I told you what he said," Stevie responded, lowering her voice. "If he goes on about Boar Boy again, that'll just confuse everyone even more."

51

"You're the best chance we have right now," Thad explained. "Louie is doing his best to keep the peace, but some of the others want to run the Davis family out of town. Tonight."

"We need to contact Nova immediately," my mom suggested.

"And how long will it take for the Clairs to process the paperwork and assign a Seer to our problem?" Thad shrugged. "The damage could already be done by then. I need help now."

My stomach was uneasy because I knew he was right.

"Stevie, I think we should go," I said.

"Darn it. I hate it when you're right." Stevie rolled her eyes. "I'll grab my purse."

Of course, the second I'd committed to the stress management challenge, the stress in my life had exploded.

Such was my life.

Chapter 7

Yogi stuck to me like glue, and I was grateful.

The sky was dark, but the shifter community was awake and full of energy. The clan of shifters that roamed Misty Key were part human and part wolf. The colorful maze of trailer homes glowed thanks to various sets of fairy lights and street lamps surrounding the basketball court and picnic tables in the center of the neighborhood.

I saw clusters of mossy trees casting shadows in the distance. We weren't far from the swamps, and that was the way the shifters liked it. They were free to be themselves without onlookers. Yogi wagged his tail as Stevie and I approached the home of Louie Stone. By day he did maintenance at the Crystal Grande Hotel, but in the magical world he was the chief of the Misty Key shifter clan and he'd known my father. The two of them had been good friends.

I glanced around and noticed that all eyes were on Stevie and me. Thad was right. The shifters were growing restless. Justice for Chetan would be served with or without the help of Detective Winter. We stopped in front of Louie's trailer. He was waiting for us and greeted us each with a hug.

"Thank you for coming. This is a very serious matter." His voice seemed to get raspier every time we met. His long, gray hair was pulled back in a ponytail.

"We understand," I answered.

"Once again, the Clairs have been kind to us," Louie announced to those who were listening. "No one will take action against anyone in this town until we've learned the truth. I promise that our fallen brother will receive the justice he deserves."

Louie dismissed everyone with a wave of his hand.

Most people listening went back inside. Some continued loitering on the gravel streets. Louie invited us inside his trailer. Thad gently touched the small of my back as he escorted me inside right behind Stevie.

"Thad," someone shouted. Thad stopped, observing a man in the distance who ran to grab our attention. "Thad, wait a minute. I want to be part of this."

"Turner, Louie said—"

"He was my brother," Turner interrupted. "You've got to let me in. I'll talk to Louie myself."

Thad nodded and stepped aside.

I'd only seen Chetan a few times and I'd never spoken to him. But he and his brother looked alike apart from the fact that Turner had a geometrical pattern shaved into the side of his head. The five of us plus Yogi crowded into Louie's one-bedroom trailer.

"Turner, is everything okay?" Louie studied him as if he could read Turner's thoughts with just one look.

"I want to hear what the psychic says," he insisted.

"We talked about this." Louie held up a hand. "You almost let your anger take control. I can't have that. I won't. I will not watch our community suffer because you and your buddies decided to do something stupid."

Turner glared at Louie, which seemed to be a bold move given Louie's status. Turner clenched his jaw. There was a fiery spark in his eyes—the same spark I noticed whenever Thad shifted from man to wolf. Turner cleared his throat, seemingly holding back words.

"Come on, Uncle," Thad chimed in. "His brother is gone and he just wants some answers." Thad slapped Turner on the back. "He won't do anything stupid, right, Turner?"

"I promise." Turner nodded. "I just need to hear from my brother one last time. Please, don't deny me that."

"Fine," Louie said. "Thad, I'm holding you accountable for this one. None of you had better lift a finger until we've learned what really happened."

"Yes, sir." Turner clenched his hands into fists. I wasn't so sure he would keep his word, especially if Chetan's ghost still claimed that he'd been killed by Boar Boy, the small-town vandal who kept popping up in the local newspaper. It made no sense.

"Okay, Stevie." Louie gestured toward his kitchen table. It sat four people, and the dark wood matched the cabinets that made up the kitchenette on the opposite side of the room. Stevie sat at the table and I sat next to her. Louie and Turner sat across from us, and Thad sat with Yogi on an adjacent loveseat.

Louie turned on a tiny brass lamp that sat on the counter. Other than that, the rest of the trailer was dark. An evening breeze rustled the trees outside, and the sounds of chatter and laughter came from the basketball court not far down the road.

Stevie took a deep breath. My heart drummed like I was back on our double date. If Stevie was anxious, she hid it well. I didn't. I took a deep breath, keeping my eyes on Stevie as she paused to meditate. I'd seen her contact the dead many times and each time had been a unique experience—good and bad. I hoped the next hour wouldn't give me nightmares for weeks.

"The best way to call Chetan is to talk about him," Stevie explained. "Share memories. If he's still hanging around Misty Key, he'll join us. I expect he is since he was taken so suddenly."

"And if that doesn't work?" Turner raised his eyebrows. The darkness made his stare much more menacing, and it gave me goosebumps.

"Oh, I think it'll work." Stevie wrinkled her nose, staring at an empty part of the room just behind Turner.

My goosebumps didn't go away.

"How many times have you done this?" Turner tilted his head, observing the tattoos on Stevie's forearm. Most of them represented Orion and her star sign.

"More than you can count," Stevie responded with confidence.

"Stevie is a very respected Seer," Louie stated. "I trust what she says and so should you."

"I don't know if *respected* is the right word," I muttered.

Stevie chuckled. "It's okay, Louie. First-timers always want proof. Chetan, tell me something about your brother that no one else knows."

Turner glanced over his shoulder. There was no one behind him. No one he could see.

"Uh, are you telling me my brother's here?" Turner's eyes went wide.

"Yeah. He's been following you around, but I'm sure you already knew that." Stevie paused, watching the empty space behind Turner's head. "He says you've been talking to him like he's still alive. He wants you to know that he heard every word."

Turner's expression didn't change. "Well, I mean, lots of people do that. So . . ."

"He also says . . ." Stevie stopped and shook her head. "No, I'm not saying that." She rolled her eyes, looking over at Thad. "I guess Chetan was quite the ladies' man."

"What did you say?" Turner leaned forward.

Stevie exhaled loudly. "Alive or dead, the rude ones never change."

"Just tell me what he said," Turner insisted.

"I don't agree with it, but he said something about a window of opportunity to get some girl?" Stevie shrugged.

"Huh?" Turner scratched the side of his head.

"Fine," Stevie muttered. "He said now is the time to make a move on Milah because she's upset about some test results and her mom is in Mobile on business."

"Oh, Chetan." Turner chuckled. "You dog."

"Milah?" Thad laughed. "That's the woman you've been pining over?"

"Shut up." Turner glared in Thad's direction.

Thad winked at Yogi.

"How about we focus on the task at hand." Louie did his best to steer the conversation in a new direction. "Stevie, ask Chetan about the night he died."

"Now's your chance, Chetan," Stevie said out loud. "Tell us what happened. And try not to freak out on me like you did last time. I could hardly understand a word you were saying."

"He's allowed to freak out," Turner insisted. "He died."

"Geez, that's weird. You two say the same things at the same time." Stevie took a deep breath. "Okay, he says he went out with Athena."

"His first mistake," Turner murmured.

Stevie narrowed her eyes. "She got mad at him because she had a dream that he cheated on her. Really? That's why she dumped chocolate bread pudding all over your shirt? Seems a little over the top unless you really were a cheater."

"Don't get me started on Athena," Turner said. "She was bad news from the beginning. I told my brother not to get involved with her. All those sirens are the same."

"Skip to the part where he went to the bathroom," I suggested.

"He says he went to the bathroom to clean off his shirt and then . . ." Stevie stopped. Her eyes went wide, and she did her best to listen intently.

The trailer fell eerily silent. Turner tilted his head as if trying to hear his brother's words himself. Yogi lowered his head, accepting a few scratches from Thad. My heart raced as I thought of the moment Stevie and I had found

58

Chetan's body. No blood. No murder weapon. No sign that he'd struggled. Just dead.

Stevie clasped her hands together, squeezing tight.

"Stevie?" Louie's voice seemed to break her trance.

"I'm sorry." She took a deep breath. "He still insists it was Boar Boy."

"What?" Turner smacked the table, fury swirling around his irises.

"I'm just repeating what he said," Stevie continued. "He said he went to the bathroom, saw a boar's face in the mirror, and then he was gone. He's just upset as we are."

"No." Turner shook his head. "It was Athena and one of her little siren spells. It had to be. There was no weapon so it must have been magic." He gritted his teeth.

"No, the call of the siren is a thing of the past," I said, remembering what I'd read about sirens while studying for my Seer license. "They've been banned from doing it for decades. Well, the ones that kill. There is more than one siren call."

"She killed him, and she has to answer for it," Turner shouted.

"Son." Louie placed a hand on his shoulder. "You promised."

Turner clenched his hands into fists. He was like a ball of fire looking for a place to land. I gulped, knowing that his frustration would only lead to more problems. There had to be a peaceful solution and if there was, it was my job to see it through.

"We'll talk to them," I blurted out.

Stevie raised her eyebrows. "We'll what?"

"We'll talk to the Davis family and get their side of the story," I explained.

"They'll just deny everything," Turner responded. "There's no way they'll ever tell you the truth."

"We have our ways of sifting through the lies," I assured him.

"I won't rest until my brother's killer pays." Turner stood, his glare even more frightening than before.

"This is how we uncover the truth," Louie told him. "Innocent until proven guilty, remember? You don't want to go accusing the wrong person of a crime like this."

"Yep," Thad chimed in. "I know that better than anyone here."

"Turner, let's speak outside." Louie followed him out the door, leaving me alone with Thad and Stevie.

"Louie won't be able to stop him for long," Thad quietly commented. "He's after blood."

"So, what do we do?" Stevie crossed her arms. "I mean, I hate to side with Mr. Psycho out there but he's right. If Athena was involved, she won't admit it. Her family won't admit it. If it was a siren call, the police will eventually call it quits. There's no murder weapon and Athena left the bar right after she dumped chocolate down her boyfriend's shirt. I'm sure she had a solid alibi."

"There is one other option," I pointed out. "One that might clear up a whole lot more than Chetan's death."

"I'm listening," Stevie replied, "and it better be a genius plan."

"It's a plan." I paused, regaining my composure. Stevie wasn't going to like what I had to say because it involved spending more time away from the bakery.

"You still haven't spit it out, and that worries me." Stevie tapped her fingers on the table, her black nail polish blending into the shadows.

"That's because she knows you'll be mad," Thad said, bowing his head. "You see, I know you Greene girls a lot better than you think."

"Is that because you stalk us a la canine?" Stevie grinned.

"I did that once, okay?" he quickly added. "And only because I don't trust your new neighbor."

"What do you have against vampires?" Stevie argued.

"I don't know. What do you have against witches?"

Stevie grunted, forcing herself to look away as Thad smiled and patted Yogi on the head.

"Settle down, you two," I interjected. "Do you want to hear my plan or not?"

"Yes, I would love to hear your thoughts on stopping Chetan's brother from tearing apart the whole town." Stevie held her hand to her ear.

"It's simple." I gulped. It wasn't simple at all. "We have to find Boar Boy."

Chapter 8

"Get up. Don't make me get the air horn."

Aqua grabbed my comforter and threw it to the floor. I muttered a few things under my breath, and Yogi jumped to his feet wagging his tail with delight.

"What time is it?"

"Five," she responded. "And I'm going to forget I heard those things you whispered. Mom would be very disappointed."

"Aqua, we should talk," I said, rolling to the other side of my bed. "When I said I wanted to start exercising, I meant a light walk after dinner or an aerobics video from the eighties that won't make me sweat."

"Stevie is already up," she responded.

"She is?"

I sat up, rubbing the sleep from my eyes.

"She told me this morning she's doing the Crawdaddy 5K. Something about earning the most points in the region."

"I'll give it a try," I replied. "But if my legs are like jelly by lunch, I might reconsider."

"Meet me outside in ten." Aqua left my room, and I dug through my drawers searching for the right clothes. I had an abundance of yoga pants, but I knew they would be drenched in sweat by the time I ran down the block. Even when the sun wasn't shining, it was still hot. I was getting more and more used to it.

I met Aqua outside wearing a T-shirt and the only pair of running shorts I could find. Aqua stretched on the front lawn while Yogi waited impatiently to start running. I hadn't exercised since moving back to Misty Key, and I was nervous that something might crack. I took a deep breath and started my stretching.

Yogi barked as two silhouettes jogged toward us. I squinted, recognizing one of them. Stevie wore a tank top and neon green running shorts. Her hair was pinned back, and I was shocked when I noticed her smiling. Junior was at her side.

"Morning," Stevie said, stopping in front of the house. She gave Junior a high five.

"Uh, morning." I paused, waiting for one of her back-handed insults that normally spilled out her mouth nonstop on Monday mornings. Stevie's smile didn't budge.

"Morning," Junior chimed in.

"Nice shorts, Junior." Aqua grinned, crossing her arms and eyeing Junior's outfit. I had a feeling he would have looked much pastier if the sun had been up.

"I had them lying around," he responded.

"I didn't know you were a runner." I took a deep breath, hoping Stevie's good mood would last all day.

"I'm not," he answered. "But I like to fly around town in the mornings before the sun comes up. I spotted Stevie and decided to join her."

"I thought I heard screeching when I let Yogi out yesterday morning." Aqua giggled. "Don't worry. I can't hear your thoughts when you change into a bat. I can only communicate with animals that are one hundred percent animal. We learned that with Thad."

"I'll keep that in mind." Junior clasped his hands in front of him, his eyes darting to Stevie for a brief second.

"Aqua, we should get started. I need to get to the bakery early so I can go over some payroll stuff."

"We only have two employees," she muttered.

"Yeah." I nudged her arm and started jogging. Yogi followed right behind me.

When Aqua finally caught on, she ran to catch up with me. I focused on my breathing, unsure how long I would last before I would need to start walking. But at least I was going to try.

Aqua smiled from ear to ear. "That guy is hooked," she commented.

The two of us turned toward Main Street, instinctively heading toward the beach. The beach was my happy place. The sound of the ocean waves had a way of soothing the chaos that went on in my head.

"Of course he's hooked. Stevie is quite the catch when she's not so cynical."

"Imagine if she was nice too." Aqua laughed. "The men in this town wouldn't stand a chance."

"I think this means she's finally ready for a new relationship."

"Oh, thank the cosmos for that," Aqua shouted. "I'm glad she wrote that letter even if she never got a response."

"Hey, now the guy knows he's a father." I slowed my pace. I was already getting tired, and beads of sweat were already trickling down my face. "He's probably still in shock about it."

"Either way, the letter was a brilliant idea." Aqua nodded. "We should have thought of that years ago."

"We didn't know who Nate was years ago."

"Poor Orion." Aqua took a deep breath. "At least he has us." She paused for a moment and jumped up and down.

"You sure do have lots of energy this morning," I commented. "Care to share it?"

"I can't help it." Aqua ran ahead of me, turning around and running backward so we were face to face. "I've always wanted to go to a vampire wedding."

Chapter 9

"Will you marry me?"

Stevie's eyes went wide as Ike knelt down on one knee. He stretched out a hand toward the woman he'd fallen for the moment they'd met. Luann was just as wide-eyed as Stevie. She blinked a few times, a vacant look on her face.

"Would you like sugar in your coffee, sir?" Luann tilted her head, her tan more apparent under the light. Luann spent her free time doing two things. She was either at the beach or taking pictures of her mom's new kitten named Miss Cricket.

She also had problems with her memory thanks to magic and the greedy witch that had used her as an errand girl. Luann remembered nothing about the magical world, and sometimes she forgot basic things in the human world like how to tie her shoes. Because of her chaotic past, Luann worked at the Lunar Bakery under Seer supervision. I'd also given her a pair of tennis shoes without laces.

"Oh, no." Ike stood up. "She's gone into the vortex again."

Luann stared at him before her attention was drawn to a peach pastry. "Hello, Miss Cricket."

"Well, thank you for having one of your moments during our staff meeting," Stevie commented.

I grabbed Luann's hand. The last time we'd let her wander during one of her episodes, she'd ended up selling one of the café tables to a customer. Luckily, our customers hadn't arrived yet. Stevie tapped her foot, glaring at Ike. Aqua covered her mouth, trying hard to say nothing. It didn't last long.

"A staff meeting?" Aqua commented. "Really, Ike? I told you to do it somewhere romantic."

"A bakery is romantic," he argued. "She's surrounded by cake." He rubbed his forehead. Dating had been a foreign concept to him, especially when Luann had said no. Looked like he'd done what any Wild West frontiersman would have done. He'd skipped right to marriage.

"Cake," Luann stated, her expression still eerily empty. "One slice or two." Luann stood frozen with a twisted smile on her face. Her episodes were unpredictable.

"I meant like a picnic on the beach," Aqua said. "One where you talk to her first and try not to propose."

"But we're perfect for each other. I don't understand why the three of you are so shocked." Ike shrugged. "She loves cats, and I was one for over a hundred years."

Stevie couldn't contain her laughter. "That's . . . I'm sorry." She pressed her lips together.

"I think what Stevie is trying to say is that loving a cat is a little different than loving a man," I explained.

"Just a little bit," Stevie added, holding back more laughter.

"A woman needs more than just a cuddle." I pulled Luann back toward the front of the bakery as soon as she yanked her hand away and set her sights on the kitchen.

"Yeah. We have cats for that." Stevie shook her head, regaining her composure. "Sorry, that was my last jab."

"Women today are so complicated." Ike threw his hands up in the air. "I don't get it. I have shelter. I make biscuits. I have a shotgun."

"What? Who gave you one of those?" Stevie raised her eyebrows.

"I have everything Luann could ever want," he continued.

"Ike, you can't force her to say yes. It has to be her choice and judging by the fact that she's said no to every one of your date ideas, I'm guessing proposing marriage might do more harm than good here." I took a deep breath. Watching Ike adjust to being human again had been both comical and heartbreaking at times. Most of us weren't struggling to survive, and we didn't live in the Wild West. We didn't even live in the Wild South.

"So, I'm just supposed to come into work every day and stare at something I can't have?"

"Well, don't stare," Aqua responded. "It's creepy."

"I guess I'm lucky she won't remember any of this." Ike huffed as he marched back into the kitchen.

"I've traveled through space," Luann announced. She was looking up at the ceiling and swaying from side to side. The constellations had put her in some sort of trance.

Stevie checked the time. "Oh, time for the morning coffee rush." She carefully unlocked the front doors. "Aqua, I'll help you up front until Luann snaps out of it. Ember, take Luann to your office and tell Ike to keep working on those cupcake orders for this afternoon. Okay, let's have a great Monday morning, everyone."

Stevie smiled, leaving Aqua and me speechless.

Something had changed, and I wasn't sure if it was the running or Junior.

"Stevie, are you feeling—"

"Sounds like a plan," I interjected, shaking my head at Aqua. "I'll be in the office."

I escorted Luann back through the kitchen and to my office, where Yogi was taking his morning nap. The office had belonged to my dad, and I often thought of him when I sat at his desk and performed the same daily tasks he used to perform. I urged Luann to sit down as I turned on my computer.

"Oh, a wolf." She pointed at Yogi.

"Yeah." I paid little attention. She said lots of things when her memory went wonky. It was like her brain straddled both ends of the spectrum—mortal and magical. She'd once told me she'd seen a unicorn.

"Nice wolfy," she said again.

I glanced over my shoulder and realized there was more than one *wolfy* in my office.

An animal emerged from under my desk.

Its dark coat was matted, and Yogi didn't seem to mind sharing his napping zone.

The wolf was Thad.

* * *

"So, there are bats and dogs snooping around my neighborhood at night." I sighed, realizing that living so close to the bakery was affording me less and less privacy. "Should I be worried?"

"Wait, *bats*?" Thad narrowed his eyes. "What's fang boy doing flying around at night? Is he bothering you?"

"Thad, what are you doing in my office?" I tried not to stare at his naked torso, but it wasn't easy. My heart raced, especially when he leaned forward and involuntarily flexed his pecs.

Luann had snapped out of her trance, claiming she had a horrible headache. I'd led her into the kitchen for a glass of water, and when I returned to my office, Thad had already shifted and covered himself up. Although the more he embraced his canine half, the less he seemed to care about modesty.

"Ike left the back door open," he stated.

"And you couldn't walk in and order a coffee like a normal human?"

"I'm not a normal human," he pointed out. "Ember, I think we might have a problem."

"You lost your shorts?" I teased.

"No, I was out in the swamps last night keeping an eye on Turner, and I picked up a scent."

"What kind of scent?" The last time Thad had followed an unusual scent, he'd been framed for murder. My heart pounded even more.

"A boar."

"Well, aren't there lots of boars out there in the swamps?" I asked. "Why is that so weird?"

"No, I wasn't in the swamps when I noticed it." He cleared his throat. His pecs flexed again. I focused on his eyes—the shade of hickory that reminded me of a calm and quiet forest.

"Where were you?"

"Main Street." He clenched his jaw.

I imagined a boar running wild up and down Town Square.

"That doesn't happen very often, does it?"

Thad shook his head. "Nope. But that isn't the worst part. I traced the scent to Gator's drugstore."

I wrinkled my nose, wondering if Gator was up to something.

"I'll have a word with him, but I'm pretty sure Boar Boy is just a nickname," I commented. "I doubt there's an actual boar involved in petty theft and graffiti around town."

"You don't know that for sure." Thad glanced down at Yogi, who had gone back to sleep after a brief scratch behind the ears. "This is the first time I've noticed a scent like that in town. It was a little different, not to mention I never actually saw a boar during my hunt."

"Anything helps at this point." I took a deep breath. "I'm going to see the Davises this afternoon, and—"

Crash.

A burst of adrenaline raced through my body as a loud noise interrupted me. It was followed by shouting coming from the front of the bakery. Yogi jumped to his feet, and Thad shifted back into a wolf in an instant.

I ran toward the noise, anxious as to what I might find.

I just hoped it wasn't another body.

"You self-righteous fortune tellers! I hate y'all!"

"Back away from the counter or I'm calling the cops," Stevie shouted. "And for the love of sweet tea, put that mug down. You've already broken three."

I pushed through the kitchen doors and found an angry customer armed with dishes and cutlery. Her cheeks were bright red, and she scowled the minute she saw me. I'd seen her before, and she'd been just as mad.

"Athena, what are you doing?" I asked.

"What happened to Chetan wasn't my fault," she shouted, her dirty-blonde locks flowing in front of her face. "I had nothing to do with it so you can stop telling everyone I did!" She tossed another mug, and it shattered on the bakery floor.

The only other customer in the room grabbed his pastries and hurried out the door. Stevie took a deep breath. I was surprised she hadn't given Athena a piece of her mind. Or maybe she was just warming up for her grand performance. It would be just like the time Aqua had created Stevie a dating profile and random men had started showing up at the bakery. Stevie had no idea what had been going on. When she figured it out, she'd thrown an entire tray of baked goods.

Yogi and Thad in wolf form stood right behind me. Athena gave Thad the evil eye, scrunching her glossy lips and searching for something else to throw. Ike grabbed Luann by the hand and guided her into the kitchen. Aqua guarded the register while Stevie crossed her arms, calmly waiting for Athena's next move.

"We haven't said anything about you to anyone," I clarified.

"I don't believe y'all for a minute," she yelled. "Turner blames me and he's been harassing my whole family. Y'all are supposed to be peacemakers. I'm filing a complaint with the Clairs. I hope they take away your Seer licenses!"

Athena stomped out, leaving the bakery in a mess of broken porcelain.

Thad watched her go, stalking her until she closed the bakery door behind her. Stevie bit the side of her lip as she looked down at the broken mugs. She shrugged.

"Someone grab a broom."

"Uh, are you feeling okay?" Aqua cautiously approached and held her hand to Stevie's forehead. "I think you might be coming down with something."

"What?" Stevie looked around the bakery. "She was obviously misinformed, and when she cools off we'll tell her what really happened last night." Stevie looked at Thad. "And you should run home and tell Louie about this."

"Okay, I'm convinced she's possessed or something," Aqua commented. She studied Stevie from head to toe. "Who do we call for that?"

"I'm not possessed, Aqua. I'm just fine. Do you want me to yell at you to get back to work?"

"That would be nice." Aqua raised her eyebrows.

"I just had a nice morning," she said. "That's all."

Stevie stared down at the floor and Yogi barked.

Aqua laughed, covering her mouth with her hand.

"A good morning, huh?" Aqua winked.

"Huh?" Stevie glared at Yogi. "What did he say? I hate it when you two do this."

"It's not my fault I can hear Yogi's thoughts." Aqua placed her hands on her hips. "Now, can I have the afternoon off?"

"No." Stevie tucked a strand of midnight hair behind her ear. "We're too busy this afternoon."

"Then I'll have to tell everyone what Yogi saw."

Stevie stared at Yogi. "You were spying on me?"

Yogi hid behind me.

"Oh, don't take it personally," Aqua replied. "He spies on everyone."

"*I* have nothing to hide," I added.

"Stevie does," Aqua said.

"Don't you dare." Stevie clenched her jaw. Her usual pessimistic self was beginning to make an appearance.

"Junior kissed Stevie!" Aqua shouted it as loud as she could before running into the kitchen.

My eyes went wide. "Well, that explains a lot."

Chapter 10

Elizabeth had called an emergency meeting at the Crystal Grande Hotel. I had an inkling what it was about. I'd seen the *Misty Messenger*'s Tuesday morning headline. I couldn't avoid that newspaper no matter how hard I tried. At least a handful of customers skimmed through it while sipping their morning javas and then left it lying around for someone else.

Why the Crystal Grande Ain't So Grand.

I figured Elizabeth would be furious when she saw the front page story. She'd worked hard to ease into her renovation project so the locals wouldn't pitch a fit. She'd trusted me to communicate her overall vision for the historic hotel with the Misty Key Women's Society, which I had. I'd even gotten them to put a stop to all the petitions and the floods of complaints to the mayor. Elizabeth and I had reached a middle ground. She'd agreed to preserve the southern charm that made the Crystal Grande such a hospitable and traditional tourist experience. The Carmichaels had come a long way, but it appeared they'd made a new enemy.

An out-of-towner with a grudge.

"Here comes trouble." Thad appeared out of nowhere as I strolled through the lobby. I jumped, clutching my chest.

"Oh my stars, Thad." I gasped. "I hate it when you do that."

"You're supposed to be psychic, and yet it works every time." He wore his work uniform—a navy polo with the hotel's logo that showcased his muscular forearms. He hadn't shaved, and his hair was just as shaggy as the last time I'd seen him. He must have had a long night.

"Aren't you supposed to be working?" I glanced around the lobby. The woman at reception stared down at her phone as guests walked in and out of the front entrance. The hotel lobby still had sparkling chandeliers and views of the ocean, but the lobby had been updated. The vintage couches were gone, replaced with more modern furniture. Elizabeth had even had the portrait of her husband reframed. The painting was still a prominent feature of the lobby, but I had no idea how long that would last either.

"Aren't you?"

"Emergency meeting with the lady of the castle," I joked.

"I was outside and I caught a whiff of your scent," he explained. "I just wanted to see how you were doing."

I instinctively tugged my blouse, wondering if it was possible to smell my armpits without him noticing. My heart raced. We were steps away from the very spot where he'd kissed me once. It hadn't happened again since.

"Okay, I know we're friends but maybe you should keep some things to yourself," I said. "I forget you have a sensitive nose."

"Ember, it's not a bad thing." He ran his fingers through his dark hair. "Anyway, you should know that

Louie had a long talk with Turner last night. I think he's reaching a breaking point and I don't blame him. He and Chetan were inseparable, and now Turner doesn't seem to know what to do with himself."

"I wish I had new information for you. I'm going to talk to the Davis family as soon as I have a spare minute. Although after Athena's meltdown at the bakery, I'm not sure they'll even let me in." I sighed. I hated it when I had so much on my plate that I never seemed to make any progress at all.

"Every time you and I . . ." Thad stopped himself. "Never mind."

"Yeah." I nodded. I knew what he was thinking. From the moment I'd given him a reading, I'd felt the sparks between us. He was always on my mind, but that didn't change the fact that there was always something in our way whenever we tried to kindle those sparks.

Maybe the universe had a message for me.

Maybe I was ignoring it because I didn't like it.

"I should probably get back to work. Louie is in charge of pulling up the floorboards in the library and it's quite the chore." Thad walked with me toward the dining area where Elizabeth was sure to be waiting with a cup of tea.

"The floors too?" I muttered. "I thought I'd talked her into refinishing the old hardwood."

Thad shrugged.

He walked me as far as the archway leading toward Elizabeth's table and placed his hand on my shoulder. The warmth from his palm radiated through my skin. A part of me was desperate to give our first date another try, but part of me was scared of what else might happen if we did.

"Why are you walking like that?" Thad muttered.

My torso tightened, and I made a conscious effort to straighten my posture.

"Like what?" I whispered back.

"Like you pulled a hip muscle." Thad chuckled, nudging my shoulder before walking off.

One jog and I was already sore.

Elizabeth was waiting for me. A copy of the *Misty Messenger* sat on the table. I braced myself for the worst. I had no idea what Elizabeth planned to do about Tillie, but I was sure it wasn't good. I cleared my throat, sitting across from her and clenching my hands into fists.

Elizabeth slid the paper toward me. I didn't bother touching it because I'd already read it. It painted the Carmichaels in a bad light—insinuated that their lust for money was crippling the very town that had supported them for years.

"All it would take is a phone," she calmly stated. "One phone call and that new editor is out." Elizabeth lifted her chin. "And when I mean out, I mean out of the game forever."

My cheeks went warm. Something on the front page of the paper jumped out at me. It was a number. My heart raced. I concentrated on Elizabeth as she went on about how she could ruin Tillie with the snap of her fingers. Out of the corner of my eye, I saw another number flash at me. Sometimes they never stopped until they'd proven their point.

"Look, I know what she did was harsh, but maybe you should have a talk with her first?"

Another number lit up and I couldn't ignore it. It looked as if it could have set fire to the tablecloth. I glanced down. Another seven. *Why am I seeing sevens?* Seven was the mark of a witch but there weren't any witches living in Misty Key. None that I was aware of.

"And say what?" Elizabeth argued. "I've gone down that road before, and it leads to nothing but wasted time. These nosy journalist types never have the guts to say these things to my face." She held up the newspaper and shook it.

"I guess some people prefer pen and paper," I responded.

"No, I need to scare her into leaving my family alone." Elizabeth slapped the newspaper back on the table. "That's where you come in."

"Me?" I tore my gaze away from the parade of sevens plaguing our table.

"Yes, you." She firmly nodded. Not an inch of her updo came undone. "You are going to walk straight into her office and give her a warning. In the meantime, I'm digging up as much dirt as I can on her. She needs to know that two can play this game."

"Let's start with talking to her," I replied.

Sevens. Sevens. And more sevens.

They were getting worse, which meant that something was about to happen.

A waiter ran toward us. He stopped to catch his breath, resting his hands on the edge of the table. I bit the corner of my lip. I didn't know what else to do but listen.

More sevens popped out at me as the waiter straightened and clutched his chest.

"What's the matter?" Elizabeth asked, watching the waiter in disbelief. "What's so important that you couldn't walk like a proper gentleman? The guests get panicky when they see staff members running around like that. It's bad for business."

"Sorry, ma'am," the waiter breathed. "I ran all the way here."

"I can see that."

"There has been an accident," he said.

"What?" Elizabeth jumped to her feet.

"Yes, ma'am. In the library."

Elizabeth didn't waste a second. She speed-walked out of the dining room and headed straight for the library. She didn't run, but she moved as fast as she could in heels without causing a scene. It was impressive to watch and I struggled to keep up with her.

Guests had crowded around the library, but the entrance had been blocked. Elizabeth forced a smile as she weaved through the crowd, ensuring her guests that nothing was wrong. She stepped into the library and instructed a few employees to guard the entrance. The walls had been taped for painting and all the old furniture had been cleared out. Half of the room was still covered in wood flooring and the other half was bare. I noticed a few cracks in the floor. My gaze wandered all the way to a gaping hole in the floor.

And standing in front of the hole were Thad and his uncle Louie.

"Oh, thank heavens." Elizabeth rubbed her cheek as she stared at Louie. "I thought someone had died and I can't afford to have the police lurking around the hotel again and frightening all of our guests."

"Help me," a voice sounded from below the floorboards.

Elizabeth's eyes went wide.

"Sorry, ma'am. We were pulling up floorboards, and we weren't expecting to find a hole. Bryan fell in." Louie's gray hair was tied back in a ponytail. He knelt down, studying the hole that must have sat right underneath one of the giant bookshelves that had been removed.

"Well, get him out. How deep does it even go?" Elizabeth was losing her patience. She kept her distance from the hole and from Louie.

"Oh, it's not that deep," Louie responded. "We're waiting on a rope to get him out."

"There's something down here, boss." Bryan's voice floated through the room.

"Toss it up, man," Thad called. He snuck a look in my direction.

"It's too heavy," Bryan yelled back. His voice echoed through the library.

After a few minutes of Elizabeth lecturing Louie on how to supervise his subordinates, an employee arrived with a rope. Thad made a loop and tied a knot. He lowered it down, instructing Bryan to hang on. Thad and Louie used all their weight to lift Bryan out.

"Are you hurt?" Elizabeth asked.

"No, ma'am." Bryan shook his head.

"Good," Elizabeth replied. "Pay attention next time."

Bryan set a wooden box down on the floor. It had carvings of symbols along the sides, and it gave me goosebumps. My heart pounded as Elizabeth instructed him to open the box. He did his best to force open the lid. There was something inside.

A book.

"What's this?" Bryan touched the leather spine and flipped through the pages.

"Who knows?" Elizabeth shrugged. "Look, I have bigger problems right now that need my undivided attention. Leave that thing on my desk."

I locked eyes with Louie. He must have known what it was the second he'd seen the box. But who did it belong to and how had it ended up under the floorboards at the Crystal Grande Hotel?

Sevens.

It was a spell book—one that belonged to a family of witches.

I had no idea if us finding it was a good thing or a terrible mistake.

Chapter 11

"So, what's it like to kiss a vampire?"

Aqua held a box of leftover sugar cookies. They were a peace offering for the Davis family. I rang the doorbell before Stevie had a chance to raise her voice. I smoothed my top and made sure I was smiling. Yogi stood next to me wagging his tail.

"Maybe one day I'll tell you." Stevie tried to ignore the smug look on Aqua's face.

"Just focus on being friendly," I told them. "We need this visit to go well."

"I'm always friendly." Aqua cleared her throat. She wore a sky blue sundress and next to Stevie's black T-shirt it made the two of them resemble night and day. They were.

"Well, I suggest you keep your mouth shut and let me and Ember do the talking," Stevie argued. "After all, we're Seers, and you're just here to shadow us."

"So rude." Aqua glanced down at Yogi.

The Davis family consisted of five siblings who all lived in Misty Key. They'd all been born and raised in southern Alabama, and they'd all inherited the gift of the siren—a power passed down from one generation to the next in a special ceremony after a family member passed away. Each siren clan possessed a certain number of magical gifts, which meant that not every family member wielded the ancient magic. And if there was no one to accept a magical gift, that gift would fade back into the universe. Sirens held family and tradition near and dear to their hearts, which was why I knew the Davis family would never leave town even if threatened by a rogue pack of wolves.

    A warm afternoon breeze rustled a palm tree in the front yard. Athena Davis was a daughter of the eldest Davis brother, and he lived closer to the beach than I did. Their front door was a deep ocean blue, and wind chimes hung near the peephole. A woman answered the door, studying each one of us suspiciously. Her gaze fell to Yogi.

    "What a beautiful bloodhound," the woman said, her dirty-blonde locks swaying in the breeze.

    "His name is Yogi." Aqua spoke first.

    Stevie's nostrils flared.

    "Hi, I'm Ember Greene and these are my sisters." I held out my hand. When doing Seer work, Stevie and I had a routine. I usually did all the talking—the introductions and explanations. In the meantime, Stevie surveyed the house and did all of her research via the spirit world.

    "Greene," the woman repeated. "Oh yes, I've been to your bakery. I'm Kara." Her eyes darted to the box of cookies. "You're that family of psychics. I know why you're here."

    "Hey, aren't we supposed to be the psychics?" Aqua teased.

    Stevie rolled her eyes.

    "Please excuse my sister," I said. "She's a Seer-in-training. May we come in?"

Kara took a deep breath, eyeing Yogi, the box of cookies, and then Yogi again.

"You three are lucky I'm a dog lover." She knelt down and scratched Yogi behind the ears before escorting us into the living room, which resembled the front porch with blue walls and photographs of the sea mounted on the walls. The couch and loveseat were a seashell brown and Kara didn't hesitate to pat the space next to her until Yogi joined her on the couch.

"You have a beautiful home," I said.

"Thank you." Kara directed her attention back to us. "I hope you're not here to ask us to leave it because my husband will do no such thing and neither will I."

I shook my head. "No, we just wanted to talk to you about Athena."

"My daughter isn't home," Kara responded. She clasped her hands together and played with the ring on her finger. "You'll have to excuse me, but I've never been visited by anyone associated with the Clairs before. There's never been a need."

"This is sort of unofficial Seer business," I clarified. "Just think of it as a neighborly visit to see how you're doing." I nodded at Aqua, and she set the box of sugar cookies on the coffee table. Yogi sniffed it immediately.

"We could be better," Kara said. "Please, sit down."

The three of us sat across from her. Light poured in from the window and a ceiling fan made Kara's wavy hair look even messier as strands danced across her face. She looked a bit like her daughter Athena, minus the temper.

"Is Athena still a few sugars short of a sweet tea?" Aqua asked.

"*Aqua*," Stevie muttered. She sat patiently on the other end of the couch, scanning the room as casually as she could. I wondered if she'd noticed any spirits lurking around. They were usually deceased relatives.

"Excuse me?" Kara narrowed her eyes.

"What?" Aqua shrugged. "She didn't tell you she caused a scene at the bakery?"

"Athena did what?" Kara leaned forward.

"She broke dishes and everything," Aqua continued. Some days she had no filter.

"Oh." Kara clenched her jaw. "I guess you're here to give me the bill?"

"Uh, no." I smiled, trying to explain before the conversation became heated. "Look, Mrs. Davis, I think there has been a big misunderstanding and I want to make sure I clear it up."

"I'm listening." Kara took a deep breath, and Yogi licked her forearm.

"Ahem." I looked at my older sister. "Stevie?"

"On Sunday night, I spoke to Chetan and—"

"Wait a minute," she interrupted. "Isn't he the one who died?"

"Yeah." Stevie nodded and Kara's eyes went wide.

Yogi let out a soft bark as a man entered the room. He sat down next to Kara and right away there was no denying the resemblance. He was Athena's father—the eldest Davis brother. I'd met him once before as a child, but that had been the last time I'd ever spoken to him.

"Oh, Dusty, these are the Greene sisters." Kara squeezed her husband's hand.

"Greene," Dusty repeated. He had tan lines on his cheeks from time spent in the sun wearing sunglasses.

"Yes, from Lunar Bakery," she continued.

"Of course." He nodded. "I was sorry to hear about your dad. He was a good man. I took him out on my fishing boat once."

Yogi lowered his head. He'd stuck to my dad's side every day. I knew the loss had hurt him just as much as it had hurt me, my mom, and my sisters. My dad was the one ghost Stevie had tried to reach for years with absolutely no luck. I let the memories of my past wash over me. I had to stick to our objective and that was learning Athena's side of the story.

"Yes, we all miss him," I responded, glancing over at Stevie, who was quieter than usual.

"I don't know if my wife mentioned it, but we've never been visited by Seers before." Dusty took a deep breath, claiming a spot near his wife. Yogi stayed put on the sofa.

"Not even for a reading?" Aqua's eyes went wide. Requests for readings were a common occurrence and all part of being a licensed Seer. Some of us were better at offering helpful advice than others. I was slowly getting better at mastering my gift, but it wasn't always the most reliable way to get information on demand.

"No." Dusty shook his head. "How does that even work?"

"Well, you make a formal request with the Clairs, and they send the best Seer for the job," I answered. "It depends on what sort of counsel you're looking for. We all have different gifts."

"What are your gifts then?" Dusty looked at Aqua first.

Aqua placed a hand on her chest. "I'm still in training but I'm actually a pet psychic. Yeah. I'm not very useful when it comes to humans." Aqua nudged my shoulder. "Ember is a numbers gal."

"A what?" He narrowed his eyes, studying me like I was a creature from another planet. Or a northerner.

"My psychic talent is rooted in numerology," I explained. "I interpret people and places using numbers."

"Sounds complicated." Kara patted Yogi on the back.

She was right. My gift wasn't easy to explain because it wasn't a very common one. Tapping into the infinite numbers and patterns that made up the universe required lots of experience. I was gradually getting there.

"What about you?" Dusty directed his attention at Stevie.

Stevie pulled her eyes away from a painting of the ocean on the opposite wall. She was quieter when she met new people, but never for too long. She'd hardly said a thing since we'd entered the Davises' home, which meant that she'd been in a state of deep concentration.

"My talent is a lot more straightforward," she said. "I'm a medium. I see the dead."

Dusty and Kara both looked at each other.

"It explains a lot, right?" Aqua couldn't help herself. She pursed her lips, holding back the giggling that would have surely sent Stevie over the edge. Although Stevie practically lived on the edge.

"Thank you, Aqua." Stevie glared at her.

"I take it you spoke to that dead boy?" Dusty lifted his chin, observing Stevie's every movement.

"Yes, I did." Stevie hit the palms of her hands on her thighs. Yogi jumped off the couch. "And just to clarify, I did *not* point the blame at anyone. I also didn't tell a single shifter that your daughter was responsible for anything that happened."

"Those shifters have been stalking the house at night," Kara blurted out. She blinked a few times, her breathing becoming heavy. "It's only a matter of time before they cross the line. I just know something bad is going to happen. I feel it in my bones."

A tear escaped her eye, and she buried her face in her husband's chest.

Dusty hugged his wife, trying as best as he could to soothe her.

"I hope you three can put a stop to this," Dusty stated. "The tension around here is the worst I've ever seen it. We've been nothing but friendly to Louie and his clan, but if those wolves do something stupid, I will defend myself and my family. I'll have no choice."

"Louie isn't to blame, sir," I said, holding up a hand. "It's Chetan's brother. And believe me, we're doing what we can to figure out what happened at Red's that night."

"Athena would never take a life," Dusty said, raising his voice. "Especially not with the siren's death call. It's a betrayal of her magic—good family magic."

I nodded. "I understand."

"Yes, we completely understand." Stevie stood up and nudged my shoulder. "We promise we'll do everything we can to clear the air around here. Nice meeting you both."

Kara kept her head down, wiping away more tears as Stevie shooed me toward the front door. I was confused, but I was sure she had a good reason for hurrying us back onto the street. Yogi trotted into the front yard. I waved goodbye as Stevie closed the door behind us and started speed-walking back toward Main Street.

"Wow." Aqua jogged to catch up. "Could you have been ruder?"

"They'll get over it," Stevie bluntly replied. "We have bigger problems."

"Like what?" I grabbed her wrist, forcing her to slow down. "What happened? What do you know?"

"She had a chat with one of her ghosty pals," Aqua commented. "Do you ever get tired of straddling two different worlds?"

"Not now, Aqua." I glanced down the street where Yogi had paused next to a fire hydrant.

"Athena didn't do it," Stevie stated. "I'm absolutely positive."

"How do you know?" I raised my eyebrows.

Stevie sighed. "Look, I don't want to embarrass the Davises. You two have to keep this information to yourselves because none of them will ever admit this. Not in a million years."

"I'm hooked." Aqua grinned. "What's their secret?"

"Athena has no powers," Stevie whispered.

Aqua and I exchanged looks. We were both confused.

"I saw her great-great-great-grandmother or something," Stevie admitted. "She said that the family magic has been dwindling down for years. When Athena came of age, there was nothing to pass down. I guess their family traditions are dying a slow death."

"Are you serious?" I couldn't fathom how that could've happened. How could someone let such precious magic fizzle back into the universe forever?

"They're ashamed enough as it is that they have to lie about it now," Stevie continued. "But that's the scoop. Athena didn't kill Chetan with magic because she had none, and this whole ordeal is just spotlighting the fact that the Davises aren't the powerful family of sirens they used to be. I expect they're really worried about a shifter attack because there's little they can do anymore to defend themselves."

"That's the saddest thing I've ever heard," Aqua responded.

"Yeah, and you're going to keep it yourself." Stevie crossed her arms. "I don't want to be the cause of anyone's public humiliation."

"Just mine?" Aqua added.

"Exactly." Stevie cracked a smile. "Just yours."

Chapter 12

I didn't bring Tillie a box of cookies.

I was afraid she might write about them in the *Misty Messenger*. Stevie would have marched right down to her office if she decided to comment on the taste or the texture. Besides, I wasn't trying to gain her trust. I was trying to stop her from sending the Carmichaels on a rampage.

Tillie's office was on Main Street in the heart of Misty Key's hustle and bustle. It was also a short walk away from the bakery. I wiped a bead of sweat from my brow and maneuvered around a group of tourists. The height of summer was still a busy time even though it was the hottest. I'd taken an early lunch break and had practiced a few opening lines before entering the Misty Messenger's office building. Elizabeth wanted me to warn Tillie about the consequences of her actions, but Tillie hadn't seemed like the agreeable type.

"Do you have an appointment?" The receptionist looked up.

"No, but I'm here to see Tillie."

"Who?" The woman squinted, trying to make sense of my request.

"Your boss," I answered. I walked up and down the hallway, searching for Tillie's office. The receptionist ran after me, but I didn't bother to stop. I had a giant to-do list, and I was eager to cross off an item of business so I could move on to the next one.

"Uh, don't I know you?" Tillie smirked as I walked into her office. Her desk was covered with paper and clothes littered an armchair in the corner. It appeared as if she hadn't left her office in days and maybe she really hadn't.

"I'm Ember." I shook her hand. "We met at Darlene Johnston's poker game."

"Oh, yeah. The lady with all the grandkids." She gestured toward an open chair. "Have a seat." She cleared a few things off her desk but it was still cluttered with files, papers, and a bag of green chiles.

"Are those . . . ?" I wrinkled my nose, wondering if they were from her hometown.

"Green chiles from Albuquerque," she clarified. "A guy at the drugstore hooked me up. I think y'all call him Gator or something?"

"Yep." I nodded. "If you need anything out of the ordinary, Gator is your go-to guy. I hope he didn't charge you a fortune."

"I negotiated a fair price. Now, what can I do for you?"

"I wanted to talk to you about that article you wrote," I responded. "The one about the Crystal Grande Hotel."

Tillie chuckled.

"I was wondering when I'd be contacted about that," she said. "Although I wasn't expecting to see *you*." She tucked a strand of frizzy hair behind her ear. She seemed amused, which meant that my message from Elizabeth Carmichael wouldn't make much of dent.

I took a deep breath and casually studied her office.

"Well, the Crystal Grande is an important landmark in Misty Key," I explained. "It represents the foundation of our town. It's the reason our beaches are filled with tourists every summer, and tourism is how most of us make a living around here."

"So, you want me to write a retraction?" She raised her eyebrows.

"The Carmichaels have a lot of power. I don't get why you've made it your mission to piss them off." I leaned in a little closer, spotting a paper on her desk. It was covered in numbers. I tried to relax my mind and let my psychic gift shine through. It worked best when I was in control of my emotions.

"Tell me, Ember, how did a local bakery gal end up on their payroll?" She clasped her hands in front of her, smiling in a way that made her upper lip pointed. It was an expression that sent chills down my spine.

"What do you mean?"

"I mean how much do they pay you?" She chuckled. "And just how many other people around here do they keep in their back pockets? Geez. This place is even worse than I thought."

"Worse than you thought?" I narrowed my eyes. Misty Key, Alabama, would always hold a special place in my heart. Tillie had a hidden agenda. I knew she did. I just didn't know what it was.

"The Carmichaels run the show," she said. "Tell me how that's fair. Why should the rich be allowed to control everyone around them?"

I tilted my head, focusing some more on keeping myself calm as a number on Tillie's desk jumped out at me. The universe knew her secrets. It knew everybody's secrets. And if I paid close enough attention, the universe would clue me in.

Two. Nine. Another two and a nine.

"I think you might be jumping to conclusions." I kept my gaze on the papers on her desk. The numbers were beginning to speak to me. *Twenty-nine.* I'd seen that number before when my aunt Lorraine had come for a visit. She'd just dumped her latest boyfriend after finding out he'd cheated on her with her best friend.

"I doubt that."

"Then let me explain." My perception of Tillie was slowly changing. The more the numbers pointed to failed relationships and heartbreak, the more I felt sorry for her. "Elizabeth Carmichael is renovating the hotel and to help keep the peace with the locals, she hired me as a consultant. She's made lots of compromises, and I know she cares about the town and the integrity of her hotel."

"That was well rehearsed," Tillie commented. "But I stand by what I wrote. I'm not changing a thing, and I'm not stopping until everyone knows what horrible people they are."

"I thought mixing real news with your own opinions was frowned upon in your industry." I lifted my chin.

"I'm working with facts. This has nothing to do with my past relations with the Carmichaels."

"So, you've met them before?" I raised my eyebrows.

Tillie cleared her throat. "I never said that."

"Doesn't mean it's not true."

"You're trying to put words in my mouth," she quickly responded. "It's not going to work."

My eyes darted to the picture frames leaning against the wall. One stood apart from the rest—her college diploma. I recognized the name of the university. It was in southern California. I knew the Carmichael twins had spent a lot of time there.

"It already has," I lied, hoping to stir her frustrations even more. "Tell me, which Carmichael broke your heart? Was it Jewel or Jonathon?"

Tillie's cheeks turned red.

I was on the right track.

"Whatever you think you know, it isn't true," she blurted out.

"Maybe I should start a paper of my own," I added, scratching my chin. "I'll call it the *Sandy Standard*, and I'll write about whatever's bothering me and call it news."

"Very funny."

"You put Jewel all over your website, so I'm assuming she offended you somehow." I was thinking out loud, and I didn't care. It seemed to be making Tillie more and more upset. "But she didn't recognize you at all, so . . ." It hit me all at once. *Twenty-nine. Aunt Lorraine.*

Jewel had stolen Tillie's boyfriend.

"Now you're just rambling," she replied. "You don't know what the heck you're talking about."

"Jewel stole your boyfriend," I stated.

Tillie froze.

"I think you should leave." She clenched her jaw.

I chuckled.

The heartbreak wasn't funny. I'd experienced it myself, most recently when I'd worked in New York City. My boyfriend had dumped me at our favorite restaurant. I hadn't eaten a bite of sushi since. But Tillie had fashioned an elaborate plan to sabotage Jewel's entire family. She must have been planning it for years.

"You moved here and took over the local newspaper *just* to mess with Jewel, a woman who doesn't even know what she did to you," I said. "Unbelievable. I can't imagine the amount of negativity and bad karma that runs through your veins."

"Get out!" Tillie pointed at the door.

She'd finally cracked and I'd finally figured out what made her tick.

A hatred for anything Carmichael.

Chapter 13

"I'm losing my mind." Thad rubbed his eyes again.

"Why do you think I'm here?" I replied.

The two of us stood outside Gator's drugstore. It was past Main Street and the Misty Key Marina in a part of town most frequently visited by locals. Gator's great-grandmother had been a psychic so he was aware of the magical community even though he didn't have any magical gifts of his own. But he did have a talent for the needle in the haystack, which had earned him a reputation, especially with the magical folks.

"I smelled it again," he said, scratching the side of his unshaven chin. "I smell it now."

"The boar?"

"Yes, the boar. I have to figure out where it's coming from."

Thad pushed open the door and a bell chimed. Thad and I walked toward Gator's office. I waved at Miss Betty, the local pharmacist. She looked up and smoothed aside a strand of gray hair the moment she saw Thad. He'd found her lost puppy once, and she'd shouted it from the rooftops. Little did Miss Betty know that all he'd done was sniff the evening breeze.

"Hello there, Thad," she said. "What brings you in today?"

"Just a chat with your boss." He grinned. "I'm just kidding. I know *you're* the boss around here, Miss Betty."

She laughed, hardly paying me any attention.

"Oh, you're such a hoot." She wrinkled her nose.

Gator emerged from his office. He wiped the corners of his mouth, covering his red Alabama polo in crumbs. The few times I'd surprised him in his office, he'd been watching TV.

"What's going on out here?" Gator narrowed his eyes.

Miss Betty wiped the smile from her face. "It's called friendly conversation. Much better than being glued to the television set. It must be a commercial break."

"Ouch, you tell him, Miss Betty." Thad chuckled.

Gator rolled his eyes. He finished brushing the crumbs from his shirt and tugged at his belt. His dark hair fell flat against his forehead, and he'd had the same facial hair for years—a strap of stubble that ran along his chin.

"Ember, what can I do for you? Does your mama need another one of her fancy candles?"

"No," I responded. "We need to talk to you about something else." I glanced over at Miss Betty. "Maybe we should step into your office."

I followed Gator into his office, and it was messy just like Tillie's had been. A family-size bag of chips sat on his desk, and potato chip crumbs were scattered across the floor. Gator smirked as he picked up a trinket and shook it so that it jingled. It was a necklace styled with long white pendants.

"Check this out." Gator put on the necklace and chuckled. His round belly jiggled when he laughed. "I'm Gator." He paused, waiting for us to react.

"Uh, yeah," Thad said, glancing at me. "We know."

"No, I mean the necklace," he explained. "They're gator teeth. Isn't that hilarious? A buddy of mine picked them up in Louisiana." He took off the necklace and carefully placed it on his desk. "Thad, have I ever told you the story about how I got my nickname?"

"Which story?" he teased.

The most common story of how Gator got his nickname involved an orphaned child raised in the swamps. Gator's story changed every time he told it but that didn't matter. It had been so long that most of the locals didn't even know his real name and neither had I until my mother had blurted it out in a moment of rage.

Gator was the better option.

"Okay. I see what you're getting at." Gator nodded and slowly sat down at his desk. "So, what's the emergency?" He stared right at me.

"Why do you assume this is an emergency?" I placed a hand on my chest.

"It always is when you make house calls," he explained. "Well, go on. What did I do this time? Is this about the green chiles I got for that lady at the *Misty Messenger*?" He held up his hands. "Because I had no idea folks around here don't care for her much."

"Did you charge her an arm and a leg?" I asked.

"I guess I should have."

"No, we just came to . . ." I looked at Thad. "Tell him, Thad."

Thad sniffed the air. "I'm a little confused. Why do I smell garlic?"

"Oh." Gator chuckled, opening a desk drawer. The smell intensified enough that I noticed it too. "That'll be the sauerkraut I'm fermenting in my desk."

"What?" I covered my nose.

"Well, I can't do it at home." He raised his voice. "Ma keeps complaining about the smell."

"All right. Settle down. We're not the sauerkraut police. What else have you got in here?"

"Nothing." Gator crossed his arms, his eyes widening. "Just the stinky smelly sauerkraut that happens to taste amazing on an all-beef frank."

"No wild animals then?" I said.

Thad continued sniffing the air and Gator watched in awe.

"Is he going to shift right here in front of me, because that'll be a first."

"Thad, did you catch the scent again?"

"I think so." Thad nodded.

"Working together but still not together." Gator leaned back in his chair. "You two are the worst."

"Excuse me. What is that supposed to mean?" I adjusted the hem of my blouse. I knew what he meant but at the same time, I didn't want to admit it. And I didn't want to talk about it in front of Thad. We had enough on our plates already.

"I think you know." A sly smirk lit up his face. "I see y'all at Red's all the time."

"Gator, are you keeping wild animals in the storeroom?" Thad studied every inch of his office.

Gator jumped to his feet. "No! Of course not. Are you two working for the health department now? Tell me what's going on or leave."

"I found it." Thad tilted his head toward the door.

"Found what?" Gator cleared his throat.

"Follow me." Thad left the office and headed down the hall to the storage room. I was surprised to see that it was organized with shelves and shelves of labeled boxes. Thad circled the room, his eyes studying the ceiling. I took a deep breath, fanning my face. The room was hot, and my armpits were starting to feel sticky. A faint stench wafted through my nose.

Gator stamped his foot on the concrete floor.

"Thad, get your butt out of my storeroom," he shouted. "I mean it. I'll call the cops, or the Cajun army, or worse. I'll phone up the Misty Key Women's Society."

"Where is it?" Thad responded. "I know it's here."

"That's it." Gator threw his hands up in the air.

"He's talking about a scent he's been following," I explained. "He followed it here."

"You mean like the scent of a wild animal?" Gator squinted, processing the information. "I don't keep wild animals around here. Unless Miss Betty snuck her cat into work again. I found that little furball digging around in my fishing bag. And Miss Betty had the nerve to name that thing *Cuddles*."

"Cuddles is a cute name," I pointed out. "And cats are curious by nature."

"Yeah. Whatever. You better stop your boyfriend from messing with my shelves. I just had this place organized."

"I'm sorry. Boyfriend?" I raised my eyebrows.

"You heard me," Gator muttered.

"Found it!" Thad shouted from across the room. He pulled a box off the shelf right in front of him and the stench became stronger. I covered my nose.

"Hey, cut that out." Gator moved as fast as he could to stop Thad from touching anything else. I ran right behind him, stopping dead in my tracks when I noticed something looking back at me.

The three of us were speechless.

It took me a minute to understand what I was looking at.

"Is that . . . ?" I tilted my head. I wanted to get a closer look, but I didn't want to touch the thing sitting on Gator's storage room shelf.

"Yeah," Thad answered. "It sure is. No wonder the smell confused me. It's dead."

Hidden behind a box of first aid kit supplies was the head of a wild boar. I had no idea how long it had been dead, how long it had been sitting in the back of Gator's drugstore, and how on earth he hadn't noticed the smell.

"I don't get it." I shook my head. "Why are you hiding this in here? Are you insane? Do you know how unsanitary this is?"

My mind jumped from one conclusion to the next. Each theory seemed impossible, but boars were a controversial topic in Misty Key after the streak of vandalism carried out by an unknown criminal. I studied Gator. He looked wildly confused. Then again he could have been faking it.

"I . . . uh . . ." Gator was at a loss for words. A first for him.

"Gator, please don't tell me you've been . . ." Thad scratched his nose. For him, the stench was more intense. I didn't know how he was still standing. And breathing. And talking. "Oh, I don't even know what to say."

"I do." I stepped forward. "Gator, are you Boar Boy?"

Chapter 14

"Oh, it's you." My mother scolded Gator with her eyes.

"Sorry, I didn't have much of a choice," I commented, leading Gator into the kitchen for a glass of sweet tea. Thad followed right behind him, making sure he didn't pass out on the kitchen floor. Yogi wagged his tail the moment he spotted Thad.

"All right, sit down." My mom instinctively grabbed a glass from the cupboard. "What's going on? The last time I saw you, Gator, you'd caused quite the ruckus at Town Square."

"Yes, ma'am," he said. "I promise to be on my best behavior."

My mom poured him a glass of sweet tea and grabbed a leftover croissant from the breadbox. Gator happily accepted it. He'd complained that he'd felt light-headed our entire journey. He hadn't taken the news well—the news that someone had been sneaking around the drugstore.

"Can you think straight now?" Thad crossed his arms, glaring in Gator's direction. He wasn't as convinced that Gator was innocent.

"I swear," Gator breathed. "I have *no* idea how that boar's head got into my drugstore. I swear!"

"A boar's head?" a tiny voice rang through the kitchen. Orion stood in the doorway listening intently.

Stevie stood right behind him. "Cool. Where is it? Can I see it?"

"No." Stevie's response was automatic.

"Aw. You never let me do anything fun." He hung his head.

"Staring at the head of dead boar is fun for you?" Thad asked.

"Hey, kids are curious," Stevie replied.

"Cats are too, apparently." Gator gulped down his sweet tea.

"Everybody, sit down." My mom cleared her throat, eyeing every person in the kitchen. Orion skipped to his usual seat. Stevie huffed as she sat down beside him. Yogi wagged his tail, following Thad to the chair at the other end of the table and I sat next to him.

My mom rubbed the moonstone hanging around her neck. She was normally soft-spoken—whimsical, and a little out there after Dad had passed away. But the serious look on her face brought me back to my high school years when she was a lot more hard-headed. With Stevie and Aqua constantly fighting, she had to be.

"I swear I did nothing wrong," Gator muttered.

My mom grabbed the nearest candle. She kept one of her favorite vanilla and lavender scents on the windowsill above the sink. She sniffed it, closing her eyes and taking it in. She forced a smile.

"One person at a time," she instructed. "I don't want to hear y'all talking over each other. One person may speak at a time. Now, explain to me what Gator is doing in my kitchen, Ember." She looked right at me and it gave me goosebumps.

There had been times when I'd wondered if my mother could read my mind. She learned an awful lot from her prophetic dreams. Sometimes too much. Stevie had a theory once that she was a secret mind reader who had hidden her true talent from the Clairs to avoid more time-consuming assignments. Mind reading was a rare gift.

"He's here because he was about to lose his mind," I explained.

Thad chuckled.

"Okay, I had *one* panic attack." Gator rolled his eyes. "That doesn't make me a crazy person. They're a lot more common than you think."

"One at a time." My mom smacked her hand against the kitchen table and Gator jumped. "Don't make me address you by your Christian name."

Orion giggled.

"Yes, ma'am." Gator gulped.

I cleared my throat. "Can I continue?"

My mom nodded.

"Gator is Boar Boy," Thad blurted out.

The entire kitchen broke out in chatter. Yogi barked as Gator and Thad argued about the wild boar's head at the drugstore. Orion insisted on taking a trip to Gator's storage room, and Stevie insisted that it was too close to his bedtime. I did my best to calm everyone down, but my words were lost in the chaos.

Aqua appeared in the doorway. She rubbed her eyes like she'd just woken up from a nap. The second she saw everyone arguing, she grinned and claimed an empty chair. I pulled at a strand of my caramel hair, the way Aqua had often described it, and watched my mother's cheeks turn red. I was sure she was about to explode.

"Okay, quiet down, please!" I stood, doing my best to talk over the noise.

It didn't work.

My mom got Yogi's attention and muttered something I couldn't understand. I wasn't even sure that it was English. Yogi immediately trotted to the head of the table and bared his teeth. He let out a bark that pierced my eardrums and rattled my brain. My heart raced out of control. I didn't know Yogi was capable of such a vicious noise.

The entire kitchen fell silent.

"Thank you, Yogi." My mother took control of the conversation, dismissing Yogi to return to his spot at Thad's feet. "This is what happens when all y'all quit going to church on Sunday. Look at this mess y'all have gotten into. One at a time, please. Gator, are you responsible for the vandalism happening around town?"

"No, ma'am," he responded.

"And do you know anything about that poor shifter boy who died at Red's bar?"

"No, ma'am." Gator shook his head. "I'm not Boar Boy and I'm not a murderer."

"Then what's this business I hear about a boar's head at your store?" My mother's southern accent got thicker when she was frustrated.

"I don't know how it got there." Gator shook his head repeatedly. His chest rose up and down and his breathing got heavier.

"Relax," my mom said. "There's no need to panic."

"Oh, I feel dizzy." He pressed his fist to his mouth. "Oh, I'm going to ralph."

Orion leaned forward, his eyes wide with excitement.

"You do and you clean it up yourself," my mom responded. She lit her vanilla candle and placed it on the table in front of Gator. "Take a few deep breaths."

Gator did as he was told, slowly regaining his composure.

"I guess lighting a candle really does work," Stevie murmured.

"I'm sorry, Mrs. Greene," Gator explained. "I'm just nervous. Y'all know what this means, don't you?" He took another whiff of the candle. "First the vandalism and now a death. That boar's head means I'm next."

Thad and I looked at each other.

"If I may, Ma." Stevie raised her hand. My mom nodded. "Gator, this isn't *The Godfather*. Obviously, someone hid the head there on purpose. So, the question is why would someone do that?"

"To frame him, of course," Orion responded. "That's a silly question."

"Frame him for what?"

"Boar Boy has been blamed for everything around here lately," Aqua chimed in. "I mean the vandalism and then Chetan's crazy accusations. I guess someone wants us to think that Gator is Boar Boy."

"Yeah, but isn't the name *Boar Boy* just a catchy nickname the *Misty Messenger* made up?" Thad shook his head. "We're not talking about an actual boar here."

My thoughts drifted back to what I'd seen at the drugstore. Gator was right. Finding that head had been something out of a horror film. It had scared me, confused me, and had made me think of the headlines I'd been seeing in the paper for the past month. *Boar Boy*.

Maybe something similar had happened to Chetan. Maybe what he saw right before he died had convinced him that Boar Boy had been responsible. I gulped. There was also one more thing that upped the stakes.

"Uh, there's another problem here," I said. All eyes fell on me. "The papers don't know about Chetan naming Boar Boy as his killer, which means that—"

"The killer is part of the magical community," Thad finished. "I knew it."

"And it wasn't Athena," Stevie added.

"You're sure?" Thad studied her expression.

"As sure as I see dead people."

"Who else would have wanted to kill Chetan?" Thad ran his fingers through his dark locks. "And why blame it on Boar Boy? I mean, who is Boar Boy anyway?"

"I don't know. Boar Boy could be a vandal and also a killer." Aqua took a deep breath, eyeing the vanilla candle. "*And* part of the magical community. What are the odds of that?"

"I don't think so," I commented. There was still more to the puzzle we didn't know. "I think someone took advantage of all those newspaper headlines and decided to dump Boar Boy with another crime. But the killer made a mistake."

"Really? How?" Aqua casually braided her hair so that it was out of her face.

"Let's just pretend that the boar's head we found was used to confuse Chetan when he was attacked," I explained. "Chetan was already dead when he insisted Boar Boy was to blame. The killer had to know that Stevie would be around, otherwise using the boar's head would be pointless."

"So, the killer isn't just magical," Stevie replied. "The killer knows I can talk to the dead."

"And the killer knew we would be at Red's that night," I added.

The thought gave me chills.

"I guess someone in Misty Key isn't who they say they are." Thad glanced around the table.

We were all interrupted by a knock on the front door. Yogi ran to the living room. My mom looked at me, and I got up to answer it. I wasn't expecting anyone but that didn't matter. The more we learned about the mysteries surrounding Chetan's death, the more confused I was.

I was especially confused now that I knew an imposter was lurking around the very streets I frequented.

The thought made my skin crawl.

Chapter 15

"Good. All y'all are here." Nova dropped her purse on the kitchen table.

"Nice to see you, Nova," Stevie responded. Her gaze drifted to the kitchen counter, and Yogi casually backed away until he was halfway into the laundry room.

"It's the ghost cat," Aqua muttered, noticing Yogi's odd behavior. According to Stevie, the Siamese was a tease, and she followed Nova wherever she went.

"I thought you ought to know that you're on Lady Deja's radar." Nova tucked a strand of auburn hair behind her ear. It was up in a bun like always but it wasn't as stiff.

"Is that a bad thing?" Thad asked. He was oblivious to the inner workings of the Clairs.

"Yes and no." Nova opened her purse and pulled out a folder. She opened it and scanned the contents. "And when were you going to report a lost spellbook?" Nova stared right at me.

"Oh. Sorry. I was going to eventually." I'd forgotten all about the spell book at the Crystal Grande Hotel.

"Spell book?" Stevie wrinkled her nose. Any sign of witches in the area would surely make her stomach churn.

"Yes, we found one in the library," Thad explained. "Under the floorboards."

"Witches at the Crystal Grande?" Stevie scratched the side of her head. "That can't be right."

"That book is being held in Elizabeth Carmichael's office and it's up to y'all to go and get it," Nova said, jotting a few things down. "We can't identify the owner if we can't read it."

Thad raised his hand. "And how exactly does one identify the owner?"

"Lady Deja's crystal ball, of course." Nova paused and then kept writing. "And then there's this matter with the shifters and the sirens. I hate to do this during our stress management challenge but we could use all the help we can get."

Stevie sighed. "Yep. I'll do it. Put me on the case."

"Me too," I added. "We're already asking around."

"I figured you would be." Nova cleared her throat. "You two are officially on the case. Your number one priority is making sure the shifters and the sirens get along."

"It's as simple as that," Thad added. Nova glared at him.

"If you want to help, you can tell your buddies to stick to the swamps at night." She pursed her lips. "Does anyone have any questions?"

Stevie raised her eyebrows. "Do I get extra stress points for not saying something rude right now?"

Orion covered his mouth as he giggled.

"I suggest you two start at the scene of the crime. Time is of the essence here. We need answers if we're going to keep the peace around here." Nova ignored Stevie's request.

"No to the stress points then?" Stevie placed a hand on her son's shoulder while he giggled some more. They were two peas in a pod.

Nova rolled her eyes. "My stress levels have skyrocketed since that stress challenge started. Just help me figure out what happened to the shifter." She slammed her folder shut. "And get me that spell book as soon as possible. We'll be in even more trouble if all that power falls into the wrong hands."

* * *

I sat straight up in my bed.

Yogi lifted his head. A subtle noise had woken me up. I touched my chest. My heart was racing. *Creak.* Yogi trotted to my bedroom door. The muscles in my shoulders were tense as I crept toward the door and listened carefully. *Creak.*

My torso froze.

My mind flew back to the moment I'd seen Chetan lying on the floor at Red's to the spell book at the Crystal Grande Hotel and to the boar's head at Gator's drugstore. The closer I got to the truth, the more compelled I felt to look over my shoulder every five minutes. I gripped the doorknob a little too tight.

Creak.

I gathered up the courage to peek into the hallway. It was still dark outside and the upstairs hall was ridden with shadows. A figure turned the corner at the bottom of the stairs. I balled my hands into fists. Yogi raced after it. My eyes went wide as he jogged down the stairs and disappeared.

I forced myself to go after him, hanging tight to the railing as I skipped a few steps and landed in the living room. The front door was open, revealing a purplish sky and our quiet neighborhood street. I gulped. I heard Yogi's collar jingling from outside.

I mustered every ounce of courage I had and ran after him.

"I don't know who you are but you better—"

Stevie laughed. "For the love of sweet tea, sis. You look like you've just seen a ghost."

Stevie stood on the front porch in shorts and running shoes. She leaned to one side, stretching before her morning run. I was just as wide-eyed as before when I'd thought an intruder had broken into the house.

"What are you doing?" I scanned the driveway, glancing up at the sky.

"I'm running."

"Still?" I tilted my head.

"How else am I supposed to deal with all the stress that's been dumped in our laps?" she answered. "Yes, *still*. I want that award."

"Oh. But it's the middle of the night." I took a deep breath.

"It's four thirty."

"It is?" I suddenly felt like a couch potato because I was wearing pajamas.

"Isn't there a clock in your room?" She proceeded to stretch her calves.

115

"I didn't have the chance to look at it because I thought that you were an intruder," I said, almost shouting at her. I was having trouble calming myself down. I had too much to do and not enough time to do it. My never-ending to-do list had the power to drag me down sometimes.

"Yogi would have barked." Stevie watched as Yogi pranced around the yard.

"Right." I nodded. "Well, I'm wide awake. I guess now is as good of a time as any to talk about what we're going to do today."

"*I'm* going to bake bread and fill orders."

"I mean we should go to Red's," I suggested. "Maybe one of your little ghost friends saw something that might help us."

"You say that like my little ghost friends actually cooperate," she responded.

"Don't they?"

"No." She rolled her eyes. "The spirits that like to hang around like to play games. It drives me insane, but hey, I can't blame them. They're extremely bored."

"I still think we should go to Red's," I insisted.

"Fine. We'll go to Red's. Although you have more pressing things to figure out, or have you already forgotten the spell book?" Stevie began stretching her arms.

"No." I'd put off thinking about it because I knew it would be tricky. First, I had to figure out where Elizabeth had put it and if she'd been keeping tabs on it since it had been found. And then I had to figure out a way to take it without her knowing.

"Well, I'm swamped as it is at the bakery," she continued. "Get Thad to help you."

Stevie checked her watch and adjusted her running shorts. Yogi paused, glancing at something in the driveway. Stevie smiled when Junior approached us. I wasn't surprised to see him bright-eyed and ready for a workout. He always looked like he'd just drunk a pot of coffee when the sun was down.

"Ready to go?" Junior looked at me. "Nice jammies."

"So, you two—"

"We're jogging together," Stevie finished my sentence. "Yeah. It's not a big deal. Lots of people do it."

"I see." I smiled as I crossed my arms. Stevie had turned a corner I hadn't expected, but I wasn't about to ruin it. Junior had a thing for her, and he knew all about her psychic gift. Sometimes I wondered if Stevie's ability to see the dead was what had attracted him to her in the first place.

"Bye, Ember." Stevie glared at me.

I refrained from saying anything else.

Stevie wiped the intense glare off her face in an instant as soon as Junior looked her way.

"See you at work," I shouted as the two of them jogged down the street.

I waved at Yogi to come inside the house.

I had a lot to figure out. *Maybe I should light a candle.*

Chapter 16

"Just tell me the bad news and next time don't bring me carbs."

Elizabeth turned a blind eye to the box of Bama cookies Stevie had packed for me. The sweets were supposed to be an icebreaker and the cookies were a bestseller.

"I should have insisted on chocolate croissants," I muttered. "Much fancier."

"What on earth are you talking about?" Elizabeth raised her eyebrows. Her hair was a deeper shade of golden blonde and her nails were just as shiny as the diamond studs in her ears. The two of us sat at her usual table in front of an untouched platter of finger foods. Thursday morning brunch.

"Okay." I pushed the cookies aside. "I talked to Tillie."

"Who?"

"The editor at the *Misty Messenger*," I explained. "The woman responsible for that story about the Crystal Grande and that website dedicated to your daughter's screw-ups."

"And?" Elizabeth tilted her head.

"And she's not budging," I replied.

"I guess she's one of those women that have to learn everything the hard way." Elizabeth sighed. "Great. One more thing to add to my plate."

"If I may, maybe you should talk with Jewel." I clasped my hands together and rested them on the table. I glanced down at my chipped fingernail polish—a shade of coral Aqua had talked me into. Compared to Elizabeth's spotless manicure they looked shabby.

"Why would I do that?"

"Because Tillie knows Jewel and I think there's been some miscommunication between them," I explained.

"Tell me what you're talking about, Ember, and be blunt. Sometimes you're way too formal. We've been through a lot together, you know. I think you forget that sometimes." She drummed her nails on the ivory tablecloth.

"Okay, I'll be blunt." I cleared my throat. "I think Tillie went through a really bad breakup and I think Jewel had a hand in it. She's out for revenge."

Elizabeth rubbed her forehead. "Well, that explains a lot. I know my daughter goes through boyfriends like sweet tea, but she never shares anything with me. This is going to be a disaster."

"Maybe an apology would handle it?" I threw the idea out there knowing that it was probably a silly one. Tillie was way past an apology. She was in attack mode and I doubted Jewel could say anything that would change that.

"No," Elizabeth responded. She pressed her lips together, eyeing another cucumber sandwich. Chances were high that it was too dry like the others. I hoped Elizabeth didn't decide to sample any. It would only add to the fire.

Elizabeth rubbed her eye again—this time holding back a tear.

"I'm sorry," I said quietly. "Is everything okay?"

"It's just one thing after another." She sighed. "Jewel and Jonathon have been out of control since their father passed away and I don't know what to do. I have no one to even talk to about it."

"I wish I could offer you a piece of advice." I shook my head. "My dad has been gone for years and I know my mom still has a hard time being alone."

"I guess I just have to live with it," she muttered, taking a deep breath. "Sorry, Ember. My problems have nothing to do with you. I shouldn't be telling you all this."

"It's okay."

"Where were we?" She touched a cucumber sandwich and then changed her mind. "Ah, yes. I'll talk with my daughter and see what she remembers. That's a start. In the meantime, the library is a mess. There's a problem with the new floors I ordered."

"I told you to have the old ones refinished."

"My contractor didn't order enough wood, and now the style I chose is discontinued," she explained. "Looks like you might get your way after all."

"The original floor is beautiful," I told her. "And I hope you'll do something with the wood from the old bookshelves."

"I'll think about it." A sly smile crossed her face. I pushed the box of cookies in her direction.

"Some carbs to celebrate?" I asked.

"Celebrate what?"

"That your life is like a reality TV show," I said. "It's a train wreck that people pay money to watch." I paused and waited for her reaction. She'd told me to be blunt. I guessed I would soon find out if she'd really meant it.

Elizabeth carefully selected a cookie.

"I don't know what I was thinking hiring a woman who works at a bakery." She took a tiny bite, and her smile grew wider. "Every meeting we have I'm going to get fatter and fatter."

The two of us laughed.

Elizabeth wasn't as cold-hearted as she came across. She was a single woman running a hotel. She had to be that way. The more I'd gotten to know her, the more I understood. She couldn't afford to be a doormat of any kind if she wanted to keep her business afloat. I knew all too well what it felt like to be responsible for the family's livelihood. I handled the bakery's finances just like my dad had, and it was a heavy burden to bear.

"I won't pretend that I haven't put on a few since moving back home," I commented.

"You can handle a few," she responded. "My thighs seem to get more stubborn with age."

"I've taken up running," I blurted out. I thought of my one attempt at exercising before work. My legs were still sore from it. In fact, my legs were sore from watching Stevie run. "Well, sort of."

"Good for you." Elizabeth took another bite of her cookie. "I hear that Crawdaddy 5K is just around the corner."

"You know about that?"

"I know everything that goes on around here." She chuckled. "Just like I know people say that the queen has descended from her throne every time I go into town."

I tried not to blush. I'd used that line myself once or twice.

"Is that what people say?" I took a sip of my tea, not even bothering with the sugar.

"Oh, honey, you're a horrible liar," she said. "And if you'll excuse me, I have a meeting I can't be late for." She stood, smoothing her mocha brown dress that was more fitted than the other outfits she normally wore.

I gripped the handle of my teacup tighter.

"Wait," I blurted out. "I mean, I forgot to ask you. What happened with that book you found in the library? Have you decided what to do with it?"

"Oh." She exhaled loudly, setting down the rest of her chocolatey sweet. "Some woman took it off my hands."

"What? Who?" My stomach churned. There were things in that book that could be dangerous.

"Some woman from the Misty Key Historical Society, I think it was." She fixed a stray hair that was out of place. "Yes, that's it."

"Do you happen to have a name or any contact information?" I asked, my chest starting to feel tight.

"I'm not sure," Elizabeth answered. "You'll have to check with my assistant."

Elizabeth lifted her chin, walking back toward the lobby with perfect posture.

I grabbed a leftover Bama cookie and shoved it in my mouth.

Nova wasn't going to be happy.

Because, as far as I knew, there was no Misty Key Historical Society.

Chapter 17

Stevie rolled her eyes.

"Well, that makes me feel safe at night," she muttered as she pushed open the door to Red's bar. "There's a lunatic running around town with a medieval book of spells."

"We don't know how old that book is," I said.

"It was hidden under the floor." Her eyes went wide. "It was there for a *long* time."

Red's was a local hotspot in the older part of town. It was well out of the way of tourist traffic and it had once been a women's boutique. After the boutique went out of business, it became a boating supply shop. That business had also failed. Now it was a bar with limited seating and a free drink for anyone who yelled "Roll Tide"—one drink per customer. Stevie and I used to joke that the crumbling brick building was unlucky and I didn't think we were very far off.

"I just wish we knew why."

"All witches are crazy, Ember. They've been like that for hundreds of years." Stevie walked past me, heading toward the place where we'd found Chetan.

Stevie had disliked witches ever since high school, and until recently I'd never understood why. Now that I knew the truth, I didn't blame her. She'd dated one, and then he'd sold her a lemon of a spell from the shadow network that had turned Orion's father, a paramedic named Nate, into a living dead man. Nate had never spoken to her after that. Not even after she'd finally found his address and had sent him a letter saying they had a son.

"Does the same go for vampires?" I raised my eyebrows. I couldn't resist teasing her about Junior. I knew he was the only reason she got up even earlier than usual to go for runs.

"Don't push it," she muttered.

The bar wasn't very crowded and for good reason. Happy hour didn't start for another hour. Most tables were empty, and a woman with dark wavy hair wiped down the bar. She stopped when she spotted me. Her pale green eyes reminded me of the baby sea turtles that hatched on the beach at the end of summer.

"Hi there." Marlow wiped her hands on a dish towel. "I remember you two. Can I get you something to drink?"

"Um." I glanced at Stevie. "Two sweet teas, please."

"Half and half?"

"For me, yes," I answered. Half sweetened and half unsweetened had become a regular order of mine.

"I'll take all the sugar," Stevie commented, sitting down at the bar. Her gaze wandered to the empty hallway leading to the bathrooms.

"You got it." Marlow grabbed two glasses and quickly fixed our drinks.

I nudged Stevie. "Well, are you picking up an anything?"

"Nothing." Stevie shrugged. "This place is dead. I mean, *not* dead. You know what I mean. Why don't you give it a try?"

"Me?" I placed a hand on my chest. "What exactly am I looking for? I can't see the past."

"What about that thing you did with Thad, remember?" Stevie studied my expression. Her grin took me back to the night I'd given Thad a reading while sitting at the same counter.

My heart raced just thinking about it. He'd been trying to learn more about his biological parents—his dad had passed away before arriving in Misty Key. Thad had grown up not knowing what he was until he'd traveled to southern Alabama. He hadn't gotten the chance to meet his father but his uncle Louie had been the next best thing.

During readings, I started with the first set of numbers that marked a person as soon as they were born. The date of birth. I'd seen more about Thad than I'd expected. His time in the military and his time spent wandering around the West Coast, shifting in secret and paranoid that he'd be captured and experimented on by some bogus government agency.

I'd touched him, and it had lit a spark that had arranged all of the numbers that made up his life in a sort of timeline. It had been the only time I'd been able to take my gift to another level like that. My talents had the power to do so much more and I knew that because of Thad.

But that didn't mean I could see the past week at Red's bar.

"Of course I remember. I'll never forget it." I drummed my fingers on the counter the way I'd seen Elizabeth do it thousands of times.

Marlow handed us our drinks and smiled.

"So, what do you think of Misty Key so far?" Stevie held up her drink and took a swig.

"I love the beach," Marlow replied. "Spending the summer here was a no-brainer, even though I had to take a bartending job to make rent."

"Where are you from then?" I'd seen Marlow around town but this was the first time I'd made an effort to get to know her.

"Oh, Wetumpka," she answered. "Not much to do around there. I left for college and never really went back."

"Welcome to Misty Key," Stevie said.

"I assume y'all are sisters?" Marlow looked from me to Stevie. "I see the family resemblance. I don't hear it though."

"Blame Ember," Stevie said. "She ran away to New York City and lost her southernness."

"I've gotten a lot of it back," I argued. "You have to admit that."

"OK. Fine. I'll admit it. But you still wear way too much black." Stevie took another sip of her drink. She would never let go of the fact that my wardrobe consisted of black, white, and every shade of brown. The locals were into bright colors, which made sense because of the heat.

"Every outfit I wear, she says I look like burnt toast."

"That's not true," Stevie said. "The other day you wore this purple thing that looked like muscadine jelly."

"See what I mean?" I watched Marlow cover her mouth. Our banter seemed to amuse her and I was glad. The banter was a good thing. When I'd first set foot in Misty Key after a distressing phone call from my mom almost a year ago, Stevie had hardly talked to me.

"Dang, I wish I had a sister like that," Marlow commented. "I never know what to wear."

"Oh, she doesn't actually take my advice." Stevie tugged the sleeve of my shirt. "Look. Beige, beige, and more beige."

"At least it's not black," I added.

Marlow chuckled.

"It's nice to see you two in good spirits," Marlow commented. "The past few days have been a nightmare. I met this detective who made me want to run home and cry."

"Yes, we know that one," I said.

"Yeah." Marlow paused, wiping the bar like it was an automatic reflex. "I've been feeling awful about what happened. I wish there was something I could've done. I mean, I don't even know what happened. I thought it was a heart attack or something, but the newspaper said something about murder." She stopped herself and shook her head. "I don't even want to think about it."

"Did the police ask you if you saw anything suspicious that night?" I slowly sipped my sweet tea, trying not to cringe when it tasted bland. Marlow must have given me one hundred percent unsweetened.

"They did," she answered. "Over and over again." Her pale green eyes fixated on the hallway leading to the crime scene. "I didn't see anything strange, but anyone could have walked past me. It was so busy that I could hardly keep track of all the customers and then there was the argument."

"Chetan and Athena." Stevie nodded. "Yes, we know. We saw her dump chocolate bread pudding all over his shirt."

"That was quite a show." Marlow took a deep breath. "But no. I'm talking about the argument my boss had with some woman with frizzy hair."

Stevie and I looked at each other.

"What was the argument about?" I asked the question before Stevie could.

"I don't really know," Marlow responded. "I just heard her tell my boss that he was making a big mistake. She seemed upset." She sighed, pulling herself together and smiling. "Oh, well. It had nothing to do with that fella who collapsed."

"Sure." I forced a grin and another sip of my bland iced tea.

"Did this woman look like she was in her mid-thirties with a face like a caged rat?" Stevie said unapologetically. "Not from around here?"

"Uh." Marlow stared at my glass. "Yeah. I guess you could say she did."

"Did her hair have a tint of ginger to it?" I added.

Marlow nodded. "Um, yeah. Now that you mention it, I think it did."

Stevie glared at me. "Tillie."

* * *

"I'm sure y'all know why you're here," I announced.

The kitchen table was full of bakery leftovers and every seat had been taken. Orion sat next to Stevie munching on a day-old blueberry muffin while Aqua used Yogi's back as a footrest. Thad crossed his arms, leaning back in his chair and keeping his distance from Junior. Junior sat with his shoulders back, his platinum hair blending in with the white cabinets.

"I think this calls for another lavender vanilla candle, don't you?" My mom lit a candle and placed it in the center of the table. She'd been lighting them more frequently.

"I called everyone here tonight because we have a problem," I continued.

"When do we not," Aqua muttered.

Stevie shook her head. "Always a comment for everything."

"Says the one commenting on my comment." Aqua bit the corner of her lip.

"You're lucky we have company." Stevie put her arm around Orion and tried to ignore her.

"You mean Junior," Aqua murmured.

"Yeah, why is fang boy at the table?" Thad pointed out.

Junior leaned forward. "Because fang boy lives next door."

"OK." I held my hands up, my heart pounding. "Can y'all help me out or not?"

"I'm in." Thad nodded.

"Thank you." I took a deep breath. "First, there's the missing spell book. A woman went to the hotel claiming to be from the Misty Key Historical Society and took the book with her."

"The historical society disbanded ten years ago," my mom said. "It's now part of the women's society."

"Yes, I know." I cleared my throat. "That's why I called Thad. Is there any way you can track this woman down?" I asked him.

"I would have to find her scent first." He looked around the room, his eyes settling on an extra-crispy croissant that Ike had left in the oven too long.

"Is it too late to pick up on anything in Elizabeth's office?" I crossed my fingers.

"Yes."

"*Crap.*" Stevie shook her head.

"But there's a spell that can heighten my senses," Thad explained. "Louie told me about it once. That would help me find the scent in no time."

"If only we had a spell book," Stevie recited. "Oh, wait. It's lost."

Orion giggled.

"Can't you just request one from the shadow network?" Junior clasped his bony hands together like it was no big deal.

"No," Stevie, Aqua, my mom, and I said in unison.

Yogi barked to emphasize our point.

"Geez. It was only a suggestion." Junior avoided making eye contact with any of us.

"Listen, I'll do my best," Thad said. "I'll walk by Elizabeth's office tomorrow and see what I can pick up on."

"Good." I straightened my blouse. I'd changed from beige to a lemon yellow top I'd borrowed from Aqua. "The other reason I called this meeting is because . . . um . . ." I didn't know how to word my frustrations. I knew Tillie was hiding something—something aside from the fact that she'd known the Carmichael family before she'd ever moved to Misty Key and had taken over the local newspaper.

"Oh, quit being so formal," Stevie butted in. "The chick at the *Misty Messenger* is up to something and we think she should be followed around for a while."

"Yep." I shrugged. "What she said."

"Thanks for thinking of me." Junior cleared his throat, touching the color of his button-down shirt. "Bats are stealthier than wolves."

"But smaller," Thad pointed out. "I'll do it. If it means helping catch Chetan's killer, I'm all in."

"I'm in too," Junior said. "Y'all will be wanting *useful* information."

Thad clenched his jaw and refrained from saying anything else. I was grateful, but a sudden silence enveloped the kitchen. It made my stomach churn knowing that a killer was out there and a spell book had gone missing.

My gut told me that the worst was yet to come.

A buzzing noise broke the silence. Thad reached into his pocket and answered his phone. The rest of us studied his expression, and my chest went tight when he frowned.

He nodded a few times, jumping to his feet before he finally hung up. The first thing he did was look at me, the shades of hickory in each iris bolder than before.

"That was Louie," he said. "Turner and his gang are at the beach and so are the sirens."

Chapter 18

The moon lit the ocean waves and the sugary sand. The beach was usually my happy place. The sound of the sea helped calm the chaos in my head, and the smell of the saltwater took me back to many pleasant childhood memories when my dad was still alive.

Thad grabbed my hand and pulled me closer to the shoreline where Turner and his buddies were causing a scene. The sun had gone down and there wasn't a tourist in sight. Athena stood with her arms crossed. Members of the Davis family stood at her side, including her parents, Kara and Dusty.

"Thank goodness." Louie Stone stood in between in Turner and Athena. "The Seers have arrived."

"What's going on?" I rushed toward Louie, the sand scrunching in between my toes.

Stevie and I had followed Thad to the beach. Aqua, Yogi, and my mom had stayed behind with Orion, and Junior had disappeared into the night the second we'd stepped outside.

"They're terrorizing my daughter." Dusty Davis stepped forward. "We were in the middle of our monthly moonlight gathering when they showed up and started heckling us. I want this madness to stop."

"Calm down, Dusty." Louie did what he could to sound like a voice of reason. "The boys are upset and confused. Now, can we work this out peacefully?"

"I'm not confused at all." Turner stepped forward. There was rage in his eyes and I didn't have to be a shifter to notice the scent of alcohol on his breath.

Dusty pointed his finger at Turner. "You leave my daughter alone. She had *nothing* to do with your brother's death."

"Of course she did," Turner shouted. "She's a siren. She had my brother wrapped around her little finger. She seduced him and then did away with him."

"You watch your tongue, boy!" Dusty lunged forward. Thad and Louie did their best to hold him back.

A breeze drifted through the night air. I glanced up at the stars hoping an answer would come to me. An answer that would end the conflict between the sirens and the shifters. An answer that didn't involve embarrassing the Davis family by making their problems public. Nothing came to me.

I looked over my shoulder, hoping the ocean waves had been loud enough to muffle the sound of Turner shouting. I didn't want the police to get involved.

Something flickered in Turner's eyes.

"Turner, don't you dare shift." Thad's voice boomed through the night like a clap of thunder. It sent waves of electricity through my extremities. I didn't know Thad could be so firm.

"There's got to be a way we can fix this," I blurted out.

"Go ahead then. You two are supposed to be the experts." Dusty crossed his arms. With his half-buttoned Hawaiian shirt flapping in the wind, it was difficult to take him seriously.

"That's right." Stevie played along. "We've mediated lots of situations like this."

"We have?" I cleared my throat when she glared in my direction. "Yes, we have."

"First, we need to establish what each party wants," she explained.

"There's no time for your textbook mumbo-jumbo," Dusty argued. "He thinks my daughter is a murderer and she's not!"

"Can you prove it?" Turner threw his hands up in the air.

"Turner, we had a whole conversation about what happened." Stevie rubbed her forehead. "Your brother named his killer and it wasn't Athena."

"Boar Boy." Turner shouted the words like an accusation. "Boar Boy. A fictional guy the *Misty Messenger* made up. You expect me to believe that? Chetan is obviously under the influence of some kind of spell."

"We're sirens, not witches," Dusty replied. "We don't do stuff like that."

"Murderer!" Turner eyed Athena in the distance.

Athena scowled and her mother grabbed her hand and pulled her back. The group of sirens huddled together as Turner walked along the shore. My chest went tight. Visions of Turner shifting and charging at Athena raced through my mind. I feared for what might happen.

"Louie, you handle that boy or I'll handle him for you," Dusty yelled.

A scream rang through the starry night as Turner shifted from man to wolf. As a hairy canine, Turner had matted gray fur and piercing brown eyes. His teeth were pointed and the sound of him growling echoed through the night.

Stevie grabbed my hand, taking a few steps back. My eyes went wide. I wanted to look away but I couldn't; the sight of Turner as a wolf thirsty for revenge was terrifying. It left me frozen in place as my brain scrambled to come up with solutions. Kara shouted a few things as she shoved her daughter and other members of the Davis family as far away as possible.

Turner dug his barbaric paws into the sand.

"Turner!" Louie's gray ponytail was shiny under the starlight. He stepped in between Turner and the rest of the Davis family.

But Turner seemed to have made up his mind, fixating on Athena Davis.

"Get back," Thad blurted out, nudging me closer to the street. "Both of you stay back."

Thad joined his uncle. The two of them were still in human form but I doubted they would be for very long. Dusty Davis stood firmly next to the shore. His expression hadn't changed. He was angry, and I feared what he might do if Turner didn't turn around and leave. As possibly one of the only sirens in Misty Key left with magical abilities, it was up to him to protect his entire clan. The stakes were high for him.

"Leave us alone or you'll be swimming with the fishes," Dusty shouted.

The sound of his voice seemed to upset Turner even more.

Stevie and I both yelled as Turner charged at the Davis family. In one swift movement, Thad and Louie both shifted. Thad was larger than Turner or Louie, and he ran after Turner first. Louie's silver mane matched the shade of his human hair, and as a wolf he was ageless. He ran behind Thad, letting Thad tackle Turner. Turner howled and chills went down my spine as more growling filled the night air. More wolves stalked the beach—Turner's gang.

The ocean waves weren't loud enough to drown out the screams.

The Davis family ran down the shoreline, but Dusty stayed behind. He watched Thad and Louie force Turner back toward his side of the beach. But Thad and Louie were outnumbered. Turner's gang pounced, creating a scene straight from a wildlife documentary. Wolves were on top of wolves. I heard howling, growling, and whimpering. I couldn't tell who was winning and who was injured, and my heart pounded at a thousand miles per minute. I was stunned by what I saw, wishing I could help but knowing that if I ventured too close to the scuffle I would be sorry.

A wolf broke free from the pack and eyed Dusty.

It was Turner.

"Turner, no!" Screaming was all I could do, but I instinctively ran forward. I didn't want to witness the patriarch of Misty Key's siren family being torn to pieces.

Dusty remained calm—an act I found to be next to impossible given that he was seconds from death. He opened his mouth but it wasn't to scream in terror. An enchanting melody danced through the night complementing the sound of the sea.

Dusty was singing.

It didn't take long for the ocean to respond to his call. A giant wave formed in the distance and it headed straight for Turner. It blasted across the sand, grabbing its furry victim and whisking it away to the depths of the sea. I covered my mouth, not knowing what to think. I'd never seen a wave that big.

The fighting stopped.

Dusty finished his song with a mysterious hum.

Turner's gang turned and ran along the beach and Louie ran after them.

Thad shifted back into a human.

"We had it under control," he said to Dusty.

"The sea took him back to the swamps," Dusty explained. "I've committed no crime. But next time, I can't promise anything. This was just a warning."

"There won't be a next time," Thad insisted.

Dusty gritted his teeth as he ran to catch up with the rest of his family.

Something touched my arm and I jumped.

"Sorry," Junior muttered.

"Junior?" It took me a minute to realize he'd been standing right next to us.

"I'm sorry to interrupt but I thought you should know."

139

"Know what?" Stevie placed her hands on her hips.

Thad gently touched my arm, joining our conversation.

"Oh look, the bat has been spying," Thad mumbled.

"Don't act all tough, wolfy. I'm doing your job here."

"Wolfy? Really? When's the name-calling going to stop?" Thad wiped a bead of sweat from his forehead.

"OK, I can't take this anymore," Stevie cut in. "Junior, why are you here?"

"I've been spying on that woman from the newspaper just like you asked," he responded. "I thought you might like to know she's on the move."

Chapter 19

It wasn't my first time sneaking around Main Street in the middle of the might with Thad and Junior. We'd previously done it the night of a Mardi Gras party at the Crystal Grand Hotel. Thad and Junior had been just as competitive back then. Thad ran along the quiet street trying to find Tillie's scent even though Junior had insisted he already knew where Tillie was going.

"You two are crazy," Stevie muttered.

"I'm not crazy at all," Junior insisted. "I'm doing exactly what you asked me to do."

Junior turned a corner, leading us toward the older part of town. Thad jogged ahead of us, glancing over his shoulder every few minutes. The shops on Main Street were all closed and the road was empty. I heard the faint sound of the ocean in the distance and the chirping of crickets. The stars lit the sidewalk as we hurried past the bakery.

I had no idea what we would find.

Thad stopped, waiting for the three of us to catch up.

"I've got it," he said quietly.

"I never lost it," Junior commented.

Stevie rubbed her forehead. "I don't care who has what."

Out of the corner of my eye, I saw Junior grab Stevie's hand. She didn't say anything else. I pretended I didn't notice, mostly because holding Junior's hand had stopped her from complaining. I walked ahead of them with Thad by my side. I felt the weight of his stare as we picked up our pace.

"Are you okay?" His voice was soft.

"It could have been worse," I responded.

"True." He nodded. "I've never had to fight off another shifter before. I feel weird."

"Turner will come to his senses." I looked over my shoulder. Stevie and Junior were far enough away that I couldn't hear their conversation. "He doesn't have much of a choice."

"I didn't tell him about the boar's head," Thad admitted. "I thought I was helping by keeping that information from him until we found out more. I think maybe I made a mistake."

"You did what you thought was best," I replied.

"He might not have been called to the beach if I would have told him the truth." Thad hung his head. "He's been asking me about the case every day."

"How do you know Turner wouldn't have showed up on Gator's doorstep?" I took a deep breath of the humid evening air. The two of us kept a quick pace, looking up and down the street as we jogged through another crosswalk.

"I guess I don't."

"Exactly," I said, hoping I was making him feel better. I wasn't sure that I was. "That would have been even worse because Gator isn't magical. He can't defend himself."

"Then why do I feel so guilty?" Thad shook his head. "I feel like I've let down the entire clan."

"You're not their leader. Louie is."

"Yeah, I don't know how he does it," Thad commented. "I don't know how he manages to do what he does every single day and still be sane."

"If you figure out his secret, let me know." I bit my lip, reflecting on the all the tasks I'd failed to accomplish the past few days. The number one thing weighing on my mind was Boar Boy. The answers to all my unanswered questions *had* to be Boar Boy.

I stared straight ahead and realized we'd been walking the familiar path to a place we'd all been to many times. Red's was across the street. The windows were dark and neighboring trees cast shadows over the sign out front. I squinted, noticing something moving in the distance.

"What?" As soon as I uttered the word, a figure sprinted toward the bushes.

"Hey!" Thad shouted. "Hey, stop!" He broke out in a run, grabbing the mysterious night walker while Stevie and Junior caught up with me.

"Oh, you've got to be kidding me," Stevie said, staring at the front door to Red's bar.

It had been covered with graffiti.

The paint along the brick wall was fresh—so fresh I smelled it. A can of spray paint sat next to the street lamp. I nudged it with my shoe. I couldn't believe what I was seeing. We'd caught the vandal in the middle of a job. We'd finally unmasked the identity of . . .

"Boar Boy," I stated.

Thad came walking down the sidewalk, pulling someone along behind him. Tillie looked down at her feet, refusing to look up at anyone. She was dressed in all black and her frizzy ginger locks were hidden underneath a beanie. Stevie chuckled.

"Tillie is Boar Boy." Stevie chuckled some more. "This night just keeps getting better and better."

"Let me go or I'll press charges," Tillie finally snapped at Thad, yanking her arm away.

"*You're* going to press charges?" Stevie stepped forward. "*I'm* going to press charges. Do you know how long it took Darlene to paint over the mess in front of her shop? And you had the audacity to come to our poker night."

"I don't know what you're talking about." Tillie kept a smug look on her face as she crossed her arms and casually removed her beanie. "I was out for a walk."

"And you happened to stumble upon a crime scene?" Stevie added.

"This isn't a crime scene," Tillie insisted.

"Then you won't mind if I call up my buddy at the Misty Key police department." Stevie pulled out her cell phone.

"Fine," Tillie blurted out. "How much do you want?"

"This isn't about money, Tillie." I pulled my attention away from the spray paint. "This is about your single-handed attempt at destroying a community."

"Hey, you want a local paper, you've got to sell papers," she argued. "The *Misty Messenger* has been selling more than it ever has thanks to me."

"How do you sleep at night?" Stevie muttered, taking a few more steps forward. Junior held her back.

I was just as upset as she was but that didn't change the fact that we needed answers and we needed them fast. If Tillie had been parading around as Boar Boy all along then she must have been responsible for the boar's head at Gator's drugstore. But was the boar's head involved in Chetan's demise? Had Tillie played a part in that too?

"Oh, stop trying to be all self-righteous and name your price," Tillie insisted.

"I'll name a price," I responded.

"*Ember*," Stevie scolded me.

I held up a hand, hoping she would listen and understand. We'd been presented with an opportunity and I didn't want to squander it.

"The truth." I nodded matter-of-factly. "The truth is our price. Let's stop pretending. We know you're Boar Boy. We caught you red-handed. But we promise to stay quiet about it if you answer some questions."

"And clean up this mess," Stevie added. "*And* never do it again. You'll have to find another way to sell newspapers."

"I could ruin the two of you, you know," she said, focusing on the mess of paint she'd left behind when we'd spotted her. "One little article about your family bakery is all it would take."

Thad grunted as he stepped forward.

Tillie jumped back.

"Did you hide a boar's head at Gator's drugstore?" I paused, observing the way her jaw clenched and her shoulders went stiff.

"What?" she breathed, her eyes wide like she'd seen a ghost.

"You heard me," I responded.

"How do you even know about that?" She exhaled loudly, and her chest rose up and down at a faster pace. It wasn't the reaction I'd been expecting. I thought she would admit her crimes while sporting another devilish smirk and then move on to a story about how we couldn't prove anything. Instead, she looked like she might faint.

"Answer the question, hotshot," Stevie insisted.

"It was you." Tillie pointed a finger at me. "It was you all along. I should have known."

"Huh?"

Tillie narrowed her eyes. "*You* left that disgusting head on my desk?"

"Uh, no I didn't." I shook my head. "You mean the head was meant for you?"

"Wait a minute . . . I . . . I thought someone else was trying to torture me." Her eyes filled with tears. "I don't know what kind of game you all are playing but it's not funny." She slowly backed away. "I want no part of it. I haven't been able to sleep. I haven't been able to eat because I think my food might be poisoned or something. I'll tell everyone I made Boar Boy up, OK. Just leave me alone!"

Tillie turned and ran. This time, Thad didn't chase after her. The four of us stood in shock as the sound of

Tillie's footsteps grew more and more distant. I kicked over an empty can of spray paint.

"Well, that was unexpected," Junior said, stepping out of the dark to observe the damage.

"So, someone left the boar's head in Tillie's office?" I voiced my thoughts. "And she decided to pass it on to someone else?"

"Yeah, but why Gator?" Stevie asked.

My mind jumped back to the time I'd spent in her office. "The green chiles."

"Green what?" Stevie tilted her head.

"She has been to Gator's," I explained. "That's where she got the green chiles. She must have thought he was the one who left her the boar's head. Maybe she said too much to him. I mean, I'm sure he buttered her up with those chiles from her hometown."

"If that's true then we've hit another dead end." Stevie rubbed her forehead. "We've figured out who Boar Boy is, but we're not any closer to finding Chetan's killer."

"What if it's Tillie?" Thad raised his eyebrows.

"If Tillie's the killer, why bother crying 'Boar Boy'? Chetan would have flat out told me it was Tillie, or the crazy lady from the newspaper, or just a crazy lady." Stevie clasped her hands in front of her, letting Junior wrap his lanky arm around her shoulder.

"I guess you're right." Thad cleared his throat. His gaze lingered down the street. I got the sense he was putting off heading home for as long as he could.

I placed a hand on his back. His muscles were tight.

"So, what do we do now? Call the cops?" Stevie leaned against Junior. Her comfort level around Junior had skyrocketed ever since they'd started going for morning runs.

"Or we could clean up this mess?" Thad suggested.

"No way." Stevie shook her head. "Stevie ain't cleaning up crazy lady's messes. Some of us have to work in the morning."

"I think we should give Tillie a chance to do the right thing." My suggestion was met with laughter on Stevie's part but I was serious. Tillie had admitted her mistakes and now was the time for her to make things right.

And if she didn't, then maybe we'd just scratched the surface.

Maybe Tillie was capable of much more than we realized.

After all, sometimes revenge took people down shocking paths. *Murderous* paths.

Chapter 20

Fridays were always busy. Even when a killer was at large.

Stevie and Ike had been in a frenzy all morning baking extra croissants and filling a last-minute cake order for a birthday party at the Crystal Grande Hotel. Yogi sat at my feet as I answered emails and phone messages before helping at the register. Yogi napped in my office while I greeted customers and took orders. Aqua and Luann made the coffees.

"Are there nuts in the Cosmic Carrot Cake?" My next customer stared at the flavor of the week. Stevie's experiments had led to a few favorites like Good Vibes Vanilla Cake, Healing Hummingbird Bars, and Jupiter Jam Cake. Her Cosmic Carrot had gotten just as much attention. As Stevie had put it, no one could resist a good theme.

"No," I replied. "There are enough nuts in my family already. Why add more to a cake?"

The customer chuckled. "I'll try a slice."

I finished taking the customer's order and let out a yelp when a dessert plate shattered on the floor. The sudden noise caused an uncomfortable silence to engulf the bakery. I turned around and saw Luann staring at the ceiling with a vacant expression. It was the worst timing in the world for one of her episodes. A panicked look crossed Aqua's face, and I waved at her to escort Luann out of the public eye.

"Take her to the office," I muttered. "Yogi will look after her."

Aqua's brief absence caused a line to form out the door as I tried to fill orders, make drinks, and take payments. I was a one-woman show for longer than I could handle. Luann must have required Aqua's undivided attention because at least thirty minutes passed before she came back. Even with Aqua's help, our influx of customers was overwhelming.

By the time lunch rolled around, we'd sold out of croissants, cookies, and cupcakes.

We made an executive decision to close the bakery for lunch.

I massaged my neck and collapsed onto my swivel chair. It had been one of the busiest mornings we'd had in months. I chugged as much water as I could watching Luann pet Yogi. Her memory was just starting to come back.

Yogi stood and whimpered, staring at the doorway.

"He skipped his walk this morning." Aqua leaned against the doorframe. "And Stevie skipped her run."

"We had kind of a late night," I responded.

"I heard." Aqua winked and I grabbed Yogi's leash. He was good about staying near me and not running off but the leash kept my mind at ease when Main Street was extra crowded.

"What did you hear?"

"That y'all solved a mystery," she confessed.

"Like Nancy Drew?" Luann smiled, the tan lines on her arms more prominent than ever. "Y'all should see Miss

Cricket when I hide her favorite kitty toy. Mystery solved in less than five minutes."

"Luann, why don't you go grab some food," I suggested.

Luann twirled a strand of dirty-blonde hair. "It has been a while since I've had a Fat Burger what with Mama's blood pressure and all. The doctors say the salt is bad for her."

I nodded, happy to see that Luann was back to her normal chatty self.

"Ike would love that," Aqua commented. "I don't think he's been to Fat Burger yet."

"Ike?" Luann tilted her head as if the thought of inviting Ike along to lunch hadn't crossed her mind before.

"He's a really nice guy," I added, unsure if it would help her in the decision-making process.

"Yeah, he is," she agreed. "And so funny, always talking about horseshoes and bean tins. Sometimes I don't understand a word he's saying."

"He's not from around here." I paused, hoping she wouldn't take much longer to make up her mind.

"Yeah. OK." A twisted smile spread along her face as she flicked her hair over her shoulder and adjusted her T-shirt. "I see what y'all are trying to do and I'll play along."

As soon as Luann left my office, I ran toward the kitchen.

"Someone needs to tell Ike to play it cool," I whispered to Aqua, who was just steps behind me. "A double cheeseburger with fries is not the same as a wedding invitation."

"Got it." Aqua moved gracefully through the kitchen as Luann approached Ike about going out to lunch.

Yogi licked my fingertips. I took a deep breath and latched his leash to his collar. All seemed to be going well with Ike and Luann. I waved at Stevie as I exited through the back door. Yogi stayed by my side as I breathed in as much fresh air as I could. Yogi wagged his tail, and I let my thoughts wander as I continued to walk through town.

I'd been putting off reading the morning paper, and I was grateful that we'd been slammed at the bakery all morning. I wasn't sure what Tillie's next move would be. Would she turn herself in or would she sway the other way and write a nasty article about the Lunar Bakery? I had no evidence proving Tillie had vandalized various shops in town except my word. I doubted my word was good enough for Detective Winter.

Yogi yanked on his leash. I stopped, realizing I was about to cross the street without watching for oncoming traffic. I patted Yogi on the head and got a hold of myself. I looked around and realized my feet had carried me all the way to Red's.

Marlow, the bartender, was outside.

Scrubbing the front door.

I wiped the sweat from my forehead and headed in her direction. My cheeks were hot but it wasn't the sun or the humidity. My blood was starting to boil. Tillie hadn't confessed. She hadn't even tried to clean up her own mess. I ground my teeth watching Marlow scrub the brick building as vigorously as she was able to. I felt bad for her.

"Spray paint?" I commented.

"I had no idea paint could be this stubborn," Marlow responded.

"Did you call the police?"

"Oh, my boss already filed a thing," she answered. "The cops said there's not much they can do. They reckon it was the work of that misfit the paper keeps writing about."

"Boar Boy." Saying the name out loud made my stomach churn.

"That's the one." Marlow stopped to take a break. She took a sip from her water bottle and rustled the fabric of her T-shirt to cool herself off. "No offense, but Misty Key seemed like a much friendlier place until I decided to move here."

"Don't let Boar Boy get you down," I responded. "Misty Key is a home away from home." But Marlow's observation wasn't far from the truth. Tillie's arrival had changed everything.

"I don't know. Even the animals around here don't seem as friendly. I mean, you wouldn't believe the noises I heard last night—like wild animals at war. I think the noises were coming from the beach." She shook her head and scratched the side of her thigh. Her jean shorts were short enough that they'd look like swimsuit bottoms from far away.

I gulped and glanced down at Yogi. "That was a one-time thing. I promise."

"I hope you're right."

"I mean, I've lived here most of my life and not much has happened," I said. *Not much in the human world anyway.*

Marlow sighed and drank some more water before resuming her duties. I said my goodbyes as Yogi yanked at his collar again, leading me back toward the bakery. It felt good to walk, but the exercise wasn't enough to stop my blood from boiling. I debated marching straight into Tillie's office and calling the police myself.

I focused on my footsteps. I knew I needed proof of some kind to make a difference.

The bakery was open for business when I walked back into my office. Stevie had managed to refill the pastry cases out front, and Aqua had opened the doors, taking on new customers. I took a few bites of Stevie's cherry almond pound cake and returned to the register.

Our afternoon customers were steady, and it was a good thing. Ike and Luann were still out for lunch, and I was beginning to wonder if they'd eloped. I imagined Ike down on one knee while Luann sipped a strawberry milkshake. It was better than spending any more time or energy trying to understand the things that were going on in Tillie's head.

"Did you see the *Misty Messenger* this morning?" Aqua smoothed her braid as she wiped the counter in between customers.

"I avoided it on purpose."

"There was nothing about Boar Boy," she muttered. "When Stevie told me what happened last night, I was sure we were in for a nasty surprise. I guess not."

"There's still tomorrow." I stared down at my tan-colored sandals. They almost blended into the hardwood.

"What are you going to do if she doesn't turn herself in?" Aqua grabbed a cup and began making a coffee for herself, something she did every afternoon.

"You mean, what is Stevie going to do?" I pointed out. "She has been anti-Tillie since the moment she took over the newspaper."

"I guess we have quite the weekend ahead of us." Aqua finished making her coffee and added two sugars. "I wish I didn't have to study."

"When do you ever study?" I teased her.

"Hey, I'm a much better student than you think." She flipped her braid to one side. "Don't let the turquoise hair fool you."

"You change your hair as often as Mom paints the front door," I said, chuckling to myself. My mom had done it since were little. Our front door had always been a reflection of her mood. Lemon yellow was a sure sign that you'd be invited in for sweet tea and cookies.

"I loved that summer she painted it hot pink." Aqua stared up at the ceiling with a look of nostalgia. "Cookies for breakfast and cake for lunch. No chores. Best summer ever."

"Yep. The summer Dad surprised Mom with that trip to Europe."

"Oh yeah," Aqua replied. "That explains a lot."

The front door chimed. Our next customer strolled into the bakery and scanned every table in sight. He was average in height but sturdy in stature. The sleeves of his button-down shirt were rolled up to his elbows, revealing a few tattoos I couldn't entirely see.

"Hi there, welcome to Lunar Bakery," I greeted him. "What can I get you?"

The man looked right at me, and it gave me goosebumps. His eyes were like the ocean—a particular shade of blue I knew all too well. He observed the front counter, letting his gaze wander from my hair to the curves of my face.

I clutched my chest, feeling a little dizzy.

We'd never met, but I knew who he was.

"Uh, Ember?" Aqua joined me at the register. She pinched the side of my arm.

"I'm fine," I said quietly. The man was still staring at me. "Uh, go check on the orange rolls, will you?"

"But—"

"Just do it," I insisted.

Aqua took my hint and rushed into the kitchen, leaving me alone with the man in front of me. I wasn't sure what to say. All I could think about was my sister and my little nephew. Their lives were about to change, and I wasn't sure if it would be for the better.

"I'm looking for someone," the man finally said. "A woman down the street told me she worked here."

"I know who you're looking for," I replied. "She's in the kitchen."

"Oh." The man nodded. I studied the way his arms hung loosely at his sides, his complexion, and the way his jaw moved when he spoke. He looked completely normal and I was surprised.

"I have to say I was expecting . . . well, I'm not sure what I was expecting." I observed him some more.

The man frowned, his forehead creasing like an average man's would.

"What do you mean?" He clenched his jaw, aiming a suspicious glare in my direction.

"I have to ask," I blurted out. "Why are you here exactly? If it's to tell Stevie off, I'm going to have to ask you leave and say it all in a note instead. I don't think her heart could take it."

"How do you . . ." Nate grinned, running his fingers through his ashy brown hair. "Oh, I see. You're a psychic."

"I am," I admitted. "And Stevie is my sister."

"I see."

I outstretched a hand. "Nice to meet you, Nate. I think you're the first zombie ever to visit Misty Key, Alabama."

Chapter 21

"Sorry, we're closed. Family emergency."

I hurried to the front doors just as another customer eyed the chalkboard menu on the sidewalk. I apologized, collecting the sign and locking the door. I turned off the *Open* sign while Nate looked around the café. His gaze settled on the ceiling constellations.

"Very creative," he commented.

"My mom did them," I responded. My heart pounded and I kept an eye on the door leading into the kitchen. Aqua would be back any minute and then I'd have to explain who Nate was and what he was doing at the bakery.

"My girlfriend talks a lot about star signs. I guess psychics are into that stuff too."

Girlfriend?

"OK." I cleared my throat. "Look, I don't mean to be rude but what are you doing here?"

"I got Stevie's letter," he said, shrugging like the reason were obvious.

"What a relief." I placed my hands on my hips. My chest was tight and my cheeks felt like they were being baked in an oven. I was trying not to have a panic attack. "For a minute there, we thought you never got it because . . . I don't know . . . you never wrote back?"

"I had a lot to process. I have a son." His voice wasn't as deep as Thad's, but it was still deeper than Junior's. Nate had an air of mystery to him. I didn't know if it was just him or the fact that he was a living dead guy.

"OK." I inhaled and exhaled the way I did when I took the time to meditate. "OK." The dizzy spells were getting worse.

I sat down at the nearest table, envisioning the next hour going extremely well. The night Stevie had told me all about Nate, she'd cried. Stevie hardly ever cried. All these years, she'd felt responsible for what had happened to him. The car accident. The bad spell. The guilt had eaten away at her for ten years until she'd finally told us all her deepest secret.

And now her past had come back to haunt her.

"Whoa there." Nate dashed to the table and touched my forehead. "I'm not here to cause a scene. I'm just here to talk."

"Yeah." I breathed deep. "Yeah. I know that. It's just my sister has a tendency to fly off the handle, and my nephew has been asking about his father his whole life, and . . ."

"It's a lot to take in." Nate's voice was soothing. He patted me on the back. "Trust me. I feel like I've gone my whole life not knowing I have a son. The news knocked the wind out of me, so to speak."

"Do zombies even need air?" I shrugged. "Sorry. I just thought you would look a lot more—"

"Dead?" Nate finished. "It's all right. We're all pretty misunderstood. Understandable since there aren't many of us. Also, we refer to ourselves as *Morties*."

"I don't get it."

"No one does," he replied.

The kitchen door swung open and Aqua made her entrance. She narrowed her eyes, staring at the *Open* sign and then at me. She walked toward Nate and smiled.

"Who's this?" I knew that smile. She reserved it for the nights she spent bar hopping with her friends from the community college.

"Aqua, listen to me," I said. "What's Stevie doing? Is she in one of her moods?"

"No." Aqua kept staring at Nate. "Can I help you, handsome?"

"The *other* sister." I tilted my head toward Aqua. "Sorry about her."

"Now, that's a southern accent." Nate grinned as he shook Aqua's hand.

Aqua looked a little confused. "Do I know you? Ember, do I know him?"

"He's—"

A scream interrupted me.

Yogi came running.

Stevie had entered the room with a tray of pecan sticky buns and had dropped them on the floor. She covered her mouth with her hands, her cheeks as pale as I'd ever seen them. I jumped to my feet and grabbed Aqua by the wrist.

"Stevie." Nate stared at her in awe. His expression changed immediately. It was soft and eager.

Stevie's eyes were wide.

The bakery fell silent, minus the sound of Yogi licking frosting from the floor. Aqua grabbed his collar but Yogi was persistent. Nate took a step forward, and I waited in anticipation for Stevie's first words to the man she'd thought she'd lost all those years ago.

As the two of them stared at each other, I remembered the night Stevie had told me the story of how they'd met. A crazy night in New Orleans. A woman on the street had gone into anaphylactic shock and Nate had been the paramedic. Stevie saved the day thanks to the ghost of the woman's grandmother who'd told her where to find an EpiPen.

Nate had been an anomaly. He'd touched and saved so many lives in his profession that spirits had followed him around bringing him good fortune. And then there was the car accident. It had taken months for Stevie to realize that Nate had died after their first date. It was then that she'd contacted an old friend and had bought a resurrection spell off the shadow network.

Now, Nate was a mix of the two—living and dead.

Or a *Morty*, whatever that was.

"Is that who I think it is?" Aqua whispered.

"That's him," I muttered back.

"Isn't he supposed to be . . . rotting or something?" Aqua squinted, running into the same dilemma as me. Nate didn't look dead. The logic didn't add up.

"Stevie," Nate said again. "Stevie. Please, say something."

Stevie's midnight hair hid part of her face as she stared down at the mess on the floor. Nate took another step in her direction. I couldn't imagine what she must have been feeling. Stevie carefully knelt down and began cleaning up the pecan sticky buns. Nate rushed to help her. Stevie stopped suddenly.

"I'm so sorry." Stevie's voice was almost a whisper.
"I know." Nate studied her face with fascination.
"I'm really, really sorry." She sniffled.
"It's OK."

Stevie stood, wiping tears from her face. The tears kept coming. Aqua's jaw hung open. She'd never seen Stevie so vulnerable, but I had. Stevie shook her head, slowly inching back toward the kitchen.

Nate boldly stepped forward and wrapped his arms around her.

A warm tingle fluttered around my heart. The two of them together was a sight unlike any other. I quickly saw why they'd been attracted to each other in the first place. They were a complementary match. Stevie was pessimistic and uptight. Nate was calm and charming.

I wiped away my own tears. I couldn't help it. Stevie had waited for this moment for so long. She'd done her best to raise Orion on her own and it hadn't been easy. I knew deep down she suffered every day knowing that she would have to tell him about his father. It hadn't made it any easier that Orion had started asking about his dad more often.

"I'm sorry for what I did to you," Stevie said, sniffling some more.

"I understand a lot more now than I did back then," he told her.

Stevie took deep breaths, pulling away from Nate's embrace and putting herself back together. She stood up straight, smoothing her hair and her flour-splotched apron. As soon as she was satisfied with her appearance, she directed her attention back to the pecan sticky buns.

"A little help here, y'all." Stevie grabbed a rag and began wiping up the frosting. Yogi escaped from Aqua's grasp and resumed licking the floor.

"It's a pleasure to meet Stevie's baby daddy," Aqua commented.

"*Aqua.*" Stevie glared in her direction.

"You have nice skin," Aqua added, lightly brushing the side of Nate's forearm.

"You mean, for a dead guy?" Nate raised his eyebrows. "It stays that way as long as I feed it."

"And if you don't?" Aqua paid little attention to the group clean-up.

"I start to decay," he responded.

Aqua wrinkled her nose. "Gross."

"Aqua, do you mind? Grab the mop before a customer walks in." Stevie pointed toward the kitchen.

"I locked the doors." I tossed a few sticky buns into the trash before Yogi could get to them.

"Oh." Stevie avoided looking at Nate for longer than she had to. "Well, grab a mop anyway, Aqua. You know how I hate sticky floors."

"So, you're still just as bossy?" Nate grabbed the baking pan and handed it to me.

"Is she ever." Aqua laughed.

"Aqua, please." Stevie finished picking up the sticky buns and cleared her throat. "I assume you'll be wanting to meet Orion." She kept her eyes anywhere but on Nate. "He's at home with my mom. You never responded to my letter so I haven't told him about you. If you don't mind, I would like to talk with him first."

She clasped her hands behind her back. It took me second to notice her hands were shaking. She'd once told me that losing Orion was her greatest fear. I knew those fears had come to life the moment she'd seen Nate.

"I've got time." He nodded. "I don't expect him to accept me right away, especially because of what I am."

"Oh, the zombie stuff will make him love you even more," Aqua chimed in. "Trust me."

"Aqua. *Mop*." Stevie bit the side of her lip.

"I'm sorry I didn't write or call first, but I wanted to tell you the news in person." Nate grinned, glancing around the bakery as if it were his. "Stevie, I work for Undead Enterprises and they've approved my transfer request."

"You work where?" Aqua blurted out.

I covered her mouth so she would stop talking.

"What does that mean?" Stevie shifted her weight from one side to the other.

"It means I'm moving to Misty Key to be near my boy." He paused.

Stevie froze in place.

"Great," I said, raising my voice. "Well, that's just great, isn't it Stevie?"

"Uh." Stevie ran her fingers through her midnight hair. "I think I need to sit down for a minute." She rubbed her forehead. "Oh, wait. I have to deliver that birthday cake to the Crystal Grande."

"I'll do it," I volunteered. "You two have a lot to talk about."

It was the least I could do to help out and I imagined that Stevie's stress levels were through the roof. *Too bad I don't get points for this.*

Chapter 22

I saw Ike and Luann holding hands on my walk to the Crystal Grande. They were lost in conversation and I decided to save my lecture about skipping out on work for another time. Ike had clearly figured out how to win Luann's heart. Maybe she'd tried his famous whistle berry stew.

I gripped the cake box in my hands as I approached the hill leading to the hotel. I'd made the trip on my bike several times but each time had left me winded. Walking was no different. Thankfully, the view of the water made up for it. The emerald tide sparkled against the evening sky and seagulls flew along the shoreline.

By the time I reached the main entrance, I was huffing and puffing. I checked my delivery slip as I strolled into the lobby. The customer was staying in a room on the third floor. I headed for the elevator and absentmindedly stared at the buttons. I hit the button for the third floor and patiently waited for the doors to close.

My thoughts were stuck on Nate and Stevie. What were they talking about? What had Nate been doing for the past ten years? What was life like as a zombie, or *Morty* as he'd specified? Not knowing what was going on at the bakery made me anxious. I was even more anxious about Orion's reaction. Would he hate his mother for keeping his father a secret?

Something flashed at me. I forced myself out of my trance and focused on the Good Vibes Vanilla birthday cake in my hands. Another flash caught my eyes. It was a number. The elevator dinged, and I stepped onto the third floor. I knew from my conversations with Elizabeth that the third floor was next on the list for renovations.

I admired the floral wallpaper and the dark wooden floors as I searched for Room 303. Another number glowed along my path and I couldn't ignore it. *Seven.* My stomach churned. The last seven I'd seen had been right before the spell book was discovered in the library. It was the mark of the witch and it gave me the creeps. Sevens were never good news.

I gulped, finding the right room and knocking on the door. A familiar voice answered. The doorknob slowly turned and my eyes went wide. The room was dark apart from the light spilling in from behind closed curtains.

"*You* ordered a birthday cake?"

"What?" Tillie wrinkled her nose.

"And why is it so dark in here?" I flipped on the lights. Room 303 was a standard suite with a king-sized bed in one corner and vintage couch in the other.

Tillie played with her ginger blonde locks. "Is this another one of your games?"

I set the cake down on the dresser, retreating toward the balcony. I didn't know what to say to Tillie that didn't involve a rude remark or the type of swearing I heard from the kitchen when Stevie burned a batch of cookies.

"Take the cake." I rolled my eyes. "I don't want to talk to you."

"I don't want your stupid cake. Look, you better . . ."

She shut her mouth before she could finish her sentence. Tillie's eyes went wide and her entire body went still. I couldn't tell if she was joking or having trouble breathing. I balled my hands into fists, cautiously approaching her.

"Tillie? You okay?"

She didn't move a muscle.

She has to blink sometime.

The bathroom door creaked as it opened. The sound of clapping made my skin crawl. We hadn't been alone, and I was starting to wonder what I'd gotten myself into. Footsteps sounded right behind me.

"It worked. Check that out."

I turned around and all at once my stomach tied itself in knots. Marlow dropped a duffel bag to the floor and in her other hand, she held the missing spell book. She was dressed casually like she'd been the last time I'd seen her. I didn't understand.

"Marlow?"

"That's right." She hardly flinched, confidently opening the book and flipping through the pages. "It says here that she'll stay frozen for one hour. That's plenty of time."

"Plenty of time for what?"

Marlow eyed the cake box on the dresser. "I was expecting your sister but oh well. I'm running out of time anyway."

The sevens warned me but it didn't matter. Marlow had the spell book, and she'd baited Tillie and me into coming to a random room at the Crystal Grande alone. I was in trouble, and I needed to get out of Room 303 as soon as possible.

I bolted for the door.

The handle wouldn't move.

"I froze that too," she explained. "You can't leave until the time expires."

I tried to control my breathing as I turned to face her.

"Marlow, are you a witch?"

Marlow laughed. "Of course not."

"Then what are you?"

Marlow kicked her duffel bag and urged me to walk back into the room. I humored her but only because I had no choice. The best I could do was figure out what she wanted and try to leave in one piece.

"Open the bag," she instructed. I hesitated. "Go on. There are plenty of spells in here I've been wanting to try. Don't make me use you as an experiment."

I carefully unzipped her duffel bag. "Are you going to answer my question?"

"Tie her up," Marlow responded. "Use that chair on the balcony."

"I will when you answer my question," I insisted.

"You know who I am. You know who *we* are and what we represent." Her smirk grew wider and her pale green eyes looked more menacing than ever. I kicked myself for not suspecting her in the first place.

"I'm not very good with riddles."

"Just tie her up," Marlow said again. "I'm getting impatient."

Tillie stood frozen in the corner of the suite. It was strange to watch the way her eyes fixated on one spot, never blinking. She must have been screaming for help on the inside. She'd been horrible to the townsfolk, but she didn't deserve to be scared to death.

I followed Marlow's orders and grabbed a lounge chair from the balcony. I dragged it inside and attempted to move Tillie. It was like moving a stiff board, but eventually, I was able to bend her knees and arms so that she was sitting on the chair. I grabbed the rope from Marlow's duffel bag and wrapped it around Tillie's torso.

"There." I watched as Marlow opened the spell book and took a deep breath.

I thought back to the night at Red's where it had all started. Marlow had been there. She'd always been there. But I couldn't imagine why she would want Chetan dead. As far as I knew, the two of them weren't friends or even acquaintances.

My head craved answers, but my heart broke knowing that Tillie and I were in trouble and there was nothing I could do about it. I contemplated tackling Marlow to the floor, but I'd still be stuck in Room 303 and I'd never recited a spell before.

"Perfect." Marlow continued reading. "Now, I want you to drag her onto the balcony."

"What?"

"Yep." Marlow nodded. "Drag her onto the balcony or I'll read this fire spell. That'll really get this place cookin'."

"Marlow, what are you talking about? Why are you doing this?" My eye darted around the room. There was nothing I could use to defend myself. My gaze settled on the birthday cake. I inched toward it and pretended to study the path from the room to the balcony.

"I'm doing this for your own good," she said. "For *everyone's* own good. We should have the freedom to make our own rules. It was like that for hundreds of years until the Clairs took over."

I took another step toward the cake and paused.

She'd mentioned the Clairs. How did she know about the Clairs?

"The Clairs," I repeated softly. "You're a psychic?"

"I'm surprised it took you this long to figure it all out." She chuckled. "Do you ever use your gift for anything other than Seer work?"

"So, you're not a Seer?"

"I left that stuff behind a long time ago," she replied, still smirking. "I work for someone else."

"Who?"

"Our leader has worked hard to keep that information a secret."

I stared at the ocean, my mind connecting the dots that had always been there. Stevie and I had met a woman on our Seer retreat on Keke Island not too long ago. After several failed attempts at stealing Lady Deja's crystal ball, she'd revealed her true self. She'd been a member of the Interstellar Alliance—a Stella. It was a group of dark psychics and other magical folks dedicated to overthrowing the Clairs and putting a stop to mediation and conflict resolution. It sounded crazy, but the Stellas were in favor of using their gifts for personal gain no matter the bad karma it pushed into the universe.

I couldn't imagine life without the Clairs. It would be a life of pain and sorrow for many. A life apart from peace and harmony. It was a cause I didn't understand, but I'd heard there were other psychics out there who supported it.

"You're a Stella?"

"That's right," she confessed. "And you and your sister are interfering with my mission."

"Which is?"

"To cause an uproar in Misty Key." She placed her finger in the middle of the page as a placeholder. "So far, I've got the sirens and the shifters at each other's throats. It won't be long before one of them spills blood and then there will be no turning back."

My throat went tight.

"You killed Chetan." I took another step toward the cake.

"I was given the perfect opportunity and I took it. He got into a fight with a siren and you were there to witness it. The minute Athena dumped chocolate bread pudding on her boyfriend I knew I had to make my move."

There was no hint of remorse on her face and it made me sick.

But it also freaked me out.

It told me that Marlow was capable of much more than she let on, and I doubted that she would hesitate when it came time to claim her next victim. Was it Tillie? Was it me? And why had she hoped to lure Stevie into her trap?

"How did you do it?"

"A spell," she responded. "I bought one off the shadow network."

"And the boar's head?"

"Oh, yeah." She laughed. "Yeah. I used that to make Chetan think I was Boar Boy. I couldn't have him giving me away. I know how your sister likes to chat with the dead. I like to do it too."

I couldn't take my eyes off of Marlow. I'd never met another medium like my sister. I'd assumed they were all moody and intimidating like Stevie. They saw dead people at all hours of the day. The thought sounded exhausting and also terrifying. Marlow's demeanor hadn't been like my sister's at all. It scared me. Everything I thought I'd known about her had been wrong. What else had I been missing?

"I can't believe it," I said. "You're a medium."

"And ignoring the spirits around me so I wouldn't give myself away was exhausting." She sighed. "At least I don't have to do that anymore."

I glanced at Tillie, wondering if she'd been following our conversation.

"You killed Chetan and tricked him into thinking he'd been murdered by Boar Boy," I said. "And then you put the boar's head in Tillie's office?"

"Ding! Ding! Ding!" Her eyes lit up. "We have a winner. That was a nice touch, I think, keeping the editor of the local paper on her toes. It was obvious what she was doing. I couldn't believe she hadn't been caught. After I heard her arguing with my boss over something on the menu, I knew the bar would be next. And all in the name of our Santa Fe sliders. I guess they're a poor representation of her home state."

"So, you put the boar's head in Tillie's office and then Tillie took it to the drugstore because she thought Gator was taunting her. That only leaves me with one more question. Why are you after my sister and me?"

"You two are getting in the way," she explained. "I can't have you peacefully resolve everything that moves. The shifters and the sirens should already be at war. They're not, thanks to you."

I gritted my teeth. "Do you know how many innocent lives could have been lost for no dang good reason?"

"Now you sound like a local," she joked. "And it is a good cause. The Interstellar Alliance is one step closer to overthrowing all these corporate organizations that dictate our lives. How is that *not* a worthy cause?"

"If you kill me, I'll tell Stevie it was you." I hoped my comment would buy me some time. Marlow wasn't interested in anything but war, and that meant she was planning on knocking over the things that stood in her way.

One of them was me.

"Why do you think I ordered that cake? I was hoping Stevie would show up. But you'll do. You and this nosy newspaper lady can take the fall for everything."

"No one will believe it." I bit my lower lip. I had one chance. One chance to grab the spell book and try to unfreeze the door.

"Well, I have a spell book."

"How convenient," I added.

"Our leader is well versed in Misty Key history. This spellbook has been sitting under the hotel for hundreds of years. It belonged to a powerful coven that ruled over the gulf." She glanced down at the book.

I didn't know what sort of spell she was planning on reading next and I didn't care. I grabbed the cake box as fast as I could and opened it. In one swift movement, I smashed the cake in her face. Frosting covered her eyes and bits of cake covered her shirt.

She dropped the spell book.

I picked it up and pushed Marlow into the bathroom. I held the doorknob with one hand and searched for a spell with the other. I focused on any number I saw, doing my best to keep calm. The numbers lit up, directing me to the right page.

I read the freezing spell aloud, inserting jargon that focused on the bathroom door. When I finished, the doorknob wouldn't move. Marlow banged on the door, and I breathed a sigh of relief. I wasn't a witch, which meant that my attempt at casting spells was weak. Smaller spells worked, but more complicated ones didn't.

"Reversals," I muttered to myself while Marlow attempted to kick the door down. "I need a reversal spell."

"Let me out of here!" Marlow didn't give up. "You have no idea what you're doing!"

"I have some idea." I stopped at a transportation spell guaranteed to transport up to four people five hundred feet from the origin spot. I caught a glimpse of Tillie. The sight of her sent chills down my spine.

Bang.

The bathroom door fell off its hinges and smoke filled the room. I coughed and backed as far away as I could. I saw Marlow's figure near the doorframe. She waved her hand in front of her face as she stepped back into the room. She'd wiped the cake from her face, but chunks of Good Vibes Vanilla were smeared in her hair.

"Another little thing I picked up from the shadow network," she commented.

I panicked and recited the spell I'd found. I touched Tillie's hand and felt myself being lifted off the floor and dragged through the sky like a kite tied to the back of an airplane. Before I knew it, I was surrounded by water.

I rolled back and forth in the waves. Tillie was next to me but she couldn't move. She was still tied to her chair, and I struggled to keep her head above water and hang onto the spell book. I treaded water as fast I could, desperately searching for the shoreline. It wasn't far away. I laid Tillie on her back and kicked. A wave moved us forward. And then another. And then another.

I clawed at the sand when we finally reached land. My heart was pounding and I stopped to catch my breath. The pages of the spellbook were soggy and I carefully placed it on the sand. I wrung the seawater from my hair and fell onto the wet beach when I heard a scream.

Tillie!

Tillie had washed ashore still tied to her chair. I rushed to her side, unsure if I'd kept her head above water long enough for her to survive. Then again, I didn't know anything about the spell she was under. I didn't know if she could breathe or even needed to breathe. And when her hour was up, I didn't know if she would remember anything that had happened in Room 303.

The chaos on the hotel's private beach drew the attention of the staff.

I quickly untied Tillie and pulled her legs and arms so she was lying flat on her back. Her eyes were still open, and she had the same dumbfounded expression on her face. I had to get her back to the bakery. No amount of medical help could save her while she under the influence of magic.

Someone touched my shoulder.

"Ember, you're soaked." Thad helped me up and spotted Tillie. "Uh, what's the matter with her?"

"Magic," I confessed. "Can you help me get her to the bakery?"

"I can try."

* * *

I paced back and forth with a towel over my shoulders.

I'd borrowed one of Stevie's spare tank tops and it showed more cleavage than I was comfortable with. Tillie was still frozen on the wood floor. Her hour was almost up, and none of us knew what state she would be in when she had control of her body again.

Thad watched me walk up and down the café with Yogi at my heels. Aqua sat next to Stevie and Nate. I checked the clock. Five minutes left. Yogi paused just as someone knocked on the front door. I unlocked it and let in Nova. She marched right in carrying one of her oversized purses. Her latest one was a shade of tangerine she'd paired with a ruffled blouse.

"You were right about Marlow," Nova stated. "She's a Stella and she has run off."

"That'll keep me up at night," I replied.

"Lady Deja wants you to know that we're working around the clock trying to get new information." Nova studied Tillie. "Oh my, look at those eyes."

"One minute left," Thad commented.

All of us gathered around as Thad counted down.

When the hour was up, Tillie's body relaxed. She closed her eyes and kept them closed. I locked eyes with Thad.

"Isn't she supposed to be awake?" Aqua asked.

Nate knelt down and checked Tillie's pulse. He pressed his ear to her chest and shook his head.

The shock overcame me all at once. I hadn't been able to hold her head above water long enough. *Me*. I hadn't been prepared, and Tillie had taken the fall. My brain went foggy as I searched for the right words. Nothing came. I stumbled backward, feeling dizzy.

Thad caught me.

"I'm sorry but she's gone." Nate touched her neck one more time.

"No, she can't be." I shook my head. "No. There has got to be something we can do."

"This one is going to be hard to cover up," Nova muttered.

"We're not covering up anything because she's not dead." I realized I was shouting and not because Tillie and I had been the best of friends. It was because I didn't want Tillie's death on my conscience. I knew I would never be able to get rid of the guilt—the *what if* questions. What if I hadn't used that transportation spell? What if I hadn't entered Room 303 after seeing all those sevens? What if Stevie or Aqua had delivered that cake instead of me?

"You know, she could be right." Stevie spoke up. "I don't sense her spirit at all."

"Well then maybe there is something I can do to help her. Give me just a minute." Nate ran outside to his car and returned with a backpack. He pulled out a syringe and a tiny bottle with red liquid.

"He's pretty handy, isn't he," Aqua murmured.

Stevie pretended not to hear her.

"I've been doing research for Undead Enterprises for the past ten years." Nate carefully filled the syringe with the red liquid and screwed on a needle. "This stuff hasn't been tested on humans but I think it's safe."

"What is it?" I asked.

"It's a serum made with the same regenerative cells that are found in my blood," he explained. "Her body should be able to heal itself without all the other side effects that I experience. Of course, this will only work if there's a bit of life left in her."

"And if she's completely one hundred percent dead?" Aqua eagerly watched him work.

"She'll probably stay dead." Nate shrugged. "What do you think?" He waited for a consensus.

"Something is better than nothing," Nova responded. "Give it a try."

Nate stabbed Tillie's arm and administered the medicine.

Tillie's response was immediate. She gasped for air as she sat up and scanned the room. Her gaze eventually settled on the ceiling. Nate touched her forehead and studied her pupils. He grinned and put away his supplies.

"It's working and you have about twenty minutes before her cells are fully healed." He helped her up. Tillie continued to stare up at the ceiling. "You should get her home so she wakes up in her own bed. She might discount anything she saw or heard while she was under that spell."

"Good idea." Nova tightly gripped the strap of her purse. "I don't know who this guy is but I like him."

"He'll be staying." Aqua winked and helped Tillie to the door.

"Nice to meet you." Nate reached for Nova's hand. "I'm Nate."

Chapter 23

"I assume y'all know why I'm here."

When Nova stood in our kitchen it was rarely because she had good news. We'd been in the middle of Sunday dinner. My mom had lit just about every candle she could find, and I'd helped her make one of her specialties—chicken and cornbread casserole. I helped by chopping the onions because using any other kitchen appliance besides a microwave usually resulted in kitchen fires.

"You found Marlow?" Stevie chimed in.

"No." Nova cleared her throat. "I'm here to announce the winner of the stress management challenge."

Stevie nudged Orion, trying to keep his spirits up. Nate sat at the other end of the table. Orion's reaction to Nate hadn't been entirely pleasant and I'd been surprised. Orion stayed quiet. He'd eagerly asked about his father his entire life and now his dad was sitting at the kitchen table. But Orion had yet to warm up to him. Stevie had kept a brave face all week. She also hadn't mentioned Junior to Nate at all. I think she was waiting for all the dust to settle.

"I should have prepared a speech." Stevie stood and glanced down at Orion. He cracked a smile. "I knew I sealed the deal when I crossed the finish line at the Crawdaddy 5K yesterday."

I put my hands up. I hadn't been prepared to compete in the race although I'd been making it a habit to take Yogi for walks during lunch. That had been a good enough start for me.

"I surrender," I said. "You can have the prize. I guess you've earned it."

"Heartwarming." Nova pulled an envelope from her purse. "But you didn't win, Stevie."

"What?" She wrinkled her nose.

"I'll take that, thank you." My mom set down her glass of sweet tea and snatched her prize. "I need new frying pans."

"Mom?" Stevie scratched the side of her head.

"Sometimes I think y'all forget I live here," she said. "Silly because it's my house."

"As a former active Seer, Leila also qualified for the prize," Nova explained. "She completed almost every task on the list."

My mom nodded. "Even the yoga." She sat back down at the table, rubbing the moonstone around her neck.

The look on Stevie's face made me laugh.

"I think we're out of sweet tea." Aqua poured herself a cup, emptying the pitcher.

"There's more in the fridge in the garage," I said. "I'll get it." I jumped up and Yogi followed me out of the kitchen. Any excuse to get away for a minute while Stevie's loss settled in. I opened the garage door, letting Yogi spend some time on the front lawn before going back inside. It was a warm evening, but that didn't stop him from chasing a dragonfly that had buzzed through the bushes.

"Fresh air."

I turned and saw Nate in the doorway. His gaze followed Yogi.

"Something like that," I responded. "Is Stevie arguing with my mom?"

"No, I just thought I would let them have some privacy." His shoulders slumped a little.

I leaned against my mom's car as Yogi sprinted up and down the driveway.

"I'm sorry things didn't turn out the way you'd hoped." I didn't know if sympathizing would make a difference but it was worth a shot. He'd only been in Misty Key for a week but the more I'd gotten to know him, the more I liked him. My heart sank when his big reunion with his son hadn't been a joyous moment—a TV moment. Instead, Orion had kept his distance, not saying much at all.

"He'll come around with time," Nate answered. "It's just hard. He and Stevie have their routines, you know? I'm not sure where I fit in."

"I know he's happy you're here." I crossed my arms and hoped it was true. "I think he just needs to get used to the idea of having a dad around. *My* dad was practically the only father figure in his life. I think he's just trying to figure out how to handle all of this."

"Maybe moving here was a bad idea," he muttered. "I don't want him to feel forced to like or even let me in."

"Well, I think it's a great idea," I commented. "What better way to get to know your son than to be nearby?"

"I just hope I can find a place in time."

"Oh yes. The girlfriend. Is she a zombie too?" It was a little detail that had gone unnoticed by everyone but me. If Stevie didn't like her, that would be a problem.

"*Morty*," he corrected me. "And yes she is. I met her at work. She was one of our test subjects." Nate folded his arms. His tattoos were easier to see when he wore T-shirts.

"I've been meaning to ask you about that," I responded. "What sort of research do you do?"

"Well . . ." Nate tilted his head.

Yogi barked as someone jogged up the driveway.

Nate and I looked at each other.

"OK." Tillie stopped to catch her breath. "I can't take it anymore. Are you or aren't you some kind of witch?" She glared at me.

"Her memory is starting to return," Nate commented. He walked right up to her and touched her forehead. He proceeded to grab her wrists and examine the state of her skin.

"Who are you?" Tillie yanked her hands away. "Stop that."

Sweat dripped down her forehead and her cheeks turned bright red. The volume of her voice fluctuated as she yelled at Nate some more and turned away from Yogi. She was losing her mind. Nate grabbed her arms again and pulled her into the garage.

"Oh, this isn't good." Nate remained calm as he checked her pupils. "Yep. She's got the hunger."

"The what? What is that?" I shook my head. Yogi stood in between me and Tillie, refusing to move.

"It means the serum didn't work," he explained. "It means she was dead but the serum brought her back anyway. She's changing into a Morty."

"Tillie? A zombie?" My eyes went wide. That was the last thing Misty Key needed.

"Her hunger is getting worse," he continued. "It'll only make her more aggressive. We can't let her leave. She needs some professional help."

Yogi barked and it sent Tillie over the edge.

"You people are crazy and I'm going to prove it!" Tillie sobbed and shouted. She was a mess. She flailed her arms, screaming until she'd succeeded in punching Nate in the eye. He yelped, stumbling backward.

Tillie made her escape. She ran down the driveway, muttering to herself the entire way. Nate rubbed his eyes, watching Tillie jog down the street. He clenched his jaw and followed her before stopping in the driveway.

"I don't have time for this," he muttered.

And then he did something that made me want to toss my groceries. He gripped his forearm and started twisting. He twisted so hard that his forearm came loose and broke away from his body. There was no blood. No gore. Just flesh, muscle, and bone. I covered my mouth.

Nate hurled his forearm down the street. It hit Tillie's shoulder and grabbed onto her like it had a mind of its own. Nate watched as his arm dragged Tillie back toward the garage. His fingers flexed and Tillie resisted but the arm was strong. It wielded the strength of a full-grown man all on its own.

185

"What the?" There weren't words to describe what I was feeling.

Nate casually turned around. His cheeks went pale.

Orion was standing in the doorway.

"Uh . . . son . . ." Nate tried to hide his missing forearm but he was too late. "Please, don't tell your mother about this."

"Orion, are you okay?" I blocked his view and approached him with caution.

His mouth hung open.

"Whoa." Orion gasped. "Do that again. *Dad.*"

Chocolate Bread Pudding

Careful not to spill

1 cup heavy cream
3 cups whole milk
1 cup semi-sweet chocolate chips
1 cup milk chocolate chips + extra for sprinkling
4 eggs
1/2 cup sugar
2 teaspoons vanilla extract
1/2 teaspoon salt
1 loaf of day old bread cut into 1 inch cubes

Instructions

    Place the chocolate in a large mixing bowl. In a large saucepan, heat the heavy cream and milk until it simmers. Do not let it reach a rolling boil. Pour over the chocolate and let it sit for a few minutes. Stir until the mixture becomes a chocolate sauce. Set aside to cool.

    Combine the eggs, sugar, vanilla, and salt. Add in the chocolate sauce. Add the bread a cup at a time letting it soak in the chocolate and egg mixture. Pour the mixture into a greased 9x13 baking dish. Sprinkle additional milk chocolate chips on top to taste.

Cover the baking dish with aluminum foil and bake at 350 degrees Fahrenheit for 30 minutes. Remove the foil and bake for an additional 15-20 minutes until the edges are firm. Let the pudding cool before serving. *Enjoy!*

Acknowledgements

A special thanks to the friendly folks of Montgomery, Alabama. You know who you are. Thanks for you kindness and hospitality.

Thanks to my all of my taste testers who are down with eating sweets at a moment's notice.

Thanks Joe, Christine, and Annie.

Thanks to all of my readers. I wouldn't be here without you.

More books by A.GARDNER

Southern Psychic Sisters Mysteries
Dead and Butter
Mississippi Blood Cake
Dead Velvet Cheesecake
Lemon Meringue Die
Chocolate Dead Pudding

Bison Creek Mysteries:
Powdered Murder
Iced Spy
Frosted Bait
A Flurry of Lies

Lisa Almond Mysteries:
Donut Turn Around

Poppy Peters Mysteries:
Southern Peach Pie And A Dead Guy
Chocolate Macaroons And A Dead Groom
Bananas Foster And A Dead Mobster
Strawberry Tartlets And A Dead Starlet
Wedding Soufflé And A Dead Valet

Thanks, Y'all!

To be notified of sales and new releases, sign-up for my author newsletter by visiting **www.gardnerbooks.com** where I post fun extras. Learn more about me and what I'm working on by following me on social media:

Facebook: @gardnerbooks
Instagram: @agardnerbooks
Twitter: @agardnerbooks
Pinterest: @agardnerbooks

Made in the USA
Monee, IL
29 October 2020